I would like to acknowledge the
following persons, places, and things:

Judy Radul, Monika Herendy, Milena Jagoda,
Brian Lam, Blaine Kyllo, Dean Allen, Phillip McCrum,
Deanna Ferguson, Reid Shier, Clint Burnham, Brice Canyon,
Lynn Crosbie, Bruce LaBruce, Bruce McDonald, Noel S. Baker,
Jennifer Barclay, Antonia Hirsch, Guy Bennett, my family,
William Gibson, Checkpoint Charlie, the Literary Press Group,
Tom's Video, Videomatica, and the BC Arts Council.

Thank you.

American Whiskey Bar

A Novel

ARSENAL
PULP PRESS
Vancouver

ARSENAL PULP PRESS
103-1014 Homer Street
Vancouver, BC
Canada V6B 2W9
arsenalpulp.com

The publisher gratefully acknowledges the support of the Canada Council
for the Arts and the British Columbia Arts Council for its publishing
program, and the Government of Canada through the Book Publishing
Industry Development Program for its publishing activities.

Cover design by Solo
Interior design by cardigan.com
Cover photography by Rosalee Hiebert
Printed and bound in Canada

This is a work of fiction. Any resemblance of characters to
persons either living or deceased is purely coincidental.

CANADIAN CATALOGUING IN PUBLICATION DATA

Turner, Michael, 1962-
American whiskey bar / Michael Turner ;
with a foreword by William Gibson. — Rev. ed.

ISBN 1-55152-159-8

I. Title.
PS8589.U748A75 2004   c813'.54   c2004-901262-2

CONTENTS

Michael Turner

Foreword

I had forgotten ever having met Monika Herendy until I happened to sit opposite Michael Turner at a dinner in Vancouver last year. The topic turned to our respective plans, and he mentioned this new edition of his weirdly, somehow famously obscure screenplay. I myself am not numbered among those who claim to have actually attended a screening of *American Whiskey Bar* (nor, let me assure you, among those who have seen it but refuse to admit it). I had only vaguely understood, previously, the circumstances surrounding Michael's troubled authorship, the film's subsequent production, and his decision to publish the screenplay, thereby hoping to free himself from the psychic residue of the experience.

As he spoke, I found myself remembering a young Hungarian director I had met at the 1994 Cannes Film Festival, on the evening of Quentin Tarantino's having taken the Palm d'Or for *Pulp Fiction*.

When I interrupted, to described this woman to him – her heart-shaped face, her wide, full-lipped mouth, her black widow's peak, the coarse dark brows that looked as though they required constant plucking – I saw a change come over him.

Monika Herendy (for that was her name) had somehow managed to locate me through the Sony Pictures publicists under whose auspices I was in Cannes, promoting the unfinished *Johnny Mnemonic*. I had been expecting yet another interview, this one with a Hungarian journalist. Once we were seated at our table in the bar of the Hotel Majestic, however, she lost no time in introducing herself as a director, one specifically interested in my writing an adaptation of Stanislaw Lem's exceptionally enigmatic novel *The Investigation*, which she hoped to film in Portugal, she said, with primarily British financing. An intense young woman in a dark, two-piece, vaguely retro linen suit, I only found her pitch for the Lem script interesting in its impassioned vagueness. The seeming impossibility of adapting what I recalled of the material, which I had happened to read while an undergraduate, told me that I was not the writer for her project.

She had a habit of very deliberately licking the tip of an index finger, running it across one of her brows, then licking it again and running it across the other. This amounted, it seemed, to a distinctive tic. She did it many times, during the course of our half-hour together, before the Sony publicists interrupted us with their scheduling sheet, and it no doubt helped to fix her in my memory.

Looking at Michael Turner, seated opposite me in Le Crocodile last year, I found myself remembering the fixity of Monika Herendy's stare as she rose from that table in Cannes. How she tugged absently at the wrinkled front of her linen skirt as we said goodbye.

I almost expected, then, that Michael Turner might deliberately lick his finger, then smooth his brows – though of course he didn't.

He did, however, remain uncharacteristically subdued throughout the rest of our dinner, and now that I have read this book, I believe that I understand why.

William Gibson
<small>VANCOUVER, 2004</small>

American Whiskey can blend into the company of a throng
of thugs or a swarm of sophisticates. It has dog-eat-dog attitude
when need be and eloquent manners when protocol is required.
There's only one persona that American Whiskey never
adopts — it is never, ever shy or retiring.

GARY REGAN and MARDEE HAIDIN REGAN
The Book of Bourbon and Other Fine American Whiskeys

Since human beings have invented history, we have also
invented those aspects of our lives that seem most immutable, or, rather,
have invented the circumstances that determine their nature.

ANGELA CARTER
The Sadean Woman: An Exercise in Cultural History

It is true: the symbol of reality
has something reality does not have:
it does not represent any meaning
and yet it adds to it — by its very
representative nature — a new meaning.

PIER PAOLO PASOLINI
Theorem (*translated by Stuart Hood*)

My work is finished. My poet is dead.

VLADIMIR NABOKOV
Pale Fire

Preface

In the spring of 1996 I was offered a commission by the Hungarian filmmaker Monika Herendy to write a screenplay about America. The screenplay was to be based on a series of conversations Monika overheard two years before at the Cannes Film Festival. These conversations were American conversations; that is, they were undertaken by Americans – some of whom worked in the film industry, some at an Air Force base in Germany, and some just plain on vacation. The screenplay was to be called *A Bunch of Americans Talking*.

My first reaction to Monika's offer was no. No, I was not interested in writing a screenplay about America (or anything else, for that matter). I immediately wrote back, telling her that although I was flattered to be asked I really didn't have much interest in writing for the movies; not only was I ambivalent about the form but I was also ambivalent about the country. I concluded the letter with a short list of screenwriters I'd met on my travels (as well as wishing her the best of luck). I also added a PS, thanking her once again for her hospitality while I was in town (in Berlin, where we'd met the year before), extending the same offer to her if she was ever out my way, in Vancouver. And that, I thought, was that.

About three weeks later I received a second letter from Monika. She kindly thanked me for my offer of a place to stay, but was most brutal in her assessment of the screenwriters I'd put forth as possible candidates for *A Bunch of Americans Talking*. She told me that she was familiar with these writers and that she was most unimpressed with their work, noting that my ambivalence towards screenwriting was in direct proportion to her contempt for the professional screenwriter. She went on to liken the professional screenwriter to « that unfortunate baby who is born so sick that it can only respond to a doctor's formula.» In closing Monika cited a passage from the Serbian film critic Milena Jagoda, who once wrote that Cocteau was a superior filmmaker only because he was such an ordinary poet. Monika added, in her ps, that after reading my first two books, *Company Town* and *Hard Core Logo*, perhaps I, too, could one day make films like Cocteau. I was inflamed.

My dander up, I spent the next day drafting Monika a very long letter. I told her that she completely missed the formal conceits in my writing, that *Company Town* and *Hard Core Logo* were organized in verse for a reason, and that her assessment of my writing was based on a face value reading of poetry (which was one of the things I was trying to draw attention to with those first two books). I went on to elaborate how we – especially in Canada – where identity through a national literature has always been the given – are bound (indeed, suffocated!) by genre; that literary genres bring with them certain constraints, certain expecta- tions; and that these expectations limit the readings of those texts by rendering them conventional, predictable. *Company Town* and *Hard Core Logo* are both narratives that could just as easily have been written as banal realist novels. But I chose to write them in verse as an attempt to capsize the various misconceptions poetry carries (i.e., it is «difficult,» «romantic»). The idea here was to present the «simple» life of a company town in an ostensibly « difficult» structure; or, in the case of *Hard Core Logo*, contrast the boredom of a touring punk rock band with a heroic – or even epic – form. Something like that.

Monika's response was both quick and instructive. In her letter she told me that she had understood all along what I was doing with literary genre; and that she was only teasing me, trying to goad me into working with her on *A Bunch of Americans Talking*. She said that in considering my position as a «multi-genre writer, an artist who prefers to explore the possibility of ideas beyond the constraints of form, it would only follow, then, that [I] should at least entertain the idea of extending [my] hyphenated approach to other media. And what better way to do that than to collaborate with [her] on a film – the ultimate multi-media.» Monika went on to say how film is unique in that it can document a relationship between a reader and a text: you have a director negotiating a screenplay, who, in turn, translates it to actors, who, in turn, explain that translation to the audience, who, in turn, organize that translation into their own personal narratives. «So,» Monika furthered, «why not stretch out? Why not take a risk? Why not extend your writing strategies to new media, to the very place your work seems to be headed, to that place in creation that attracted me to your work in the first place?» In short, put up or shut up.

Now, given my gargantuan ego, and my inclination towards the hissy, I decided, this time, that the best thing to do would be to back off, trade in my rancour for a life-lesson. For Monika was right: it would only follow that my interest in formal innovation in writing would take me to new media forms. And although I still didn't want to write the screenplay to *A Bunch of Americans Talking*, I was, at the very least, curious about what I could do with the screenplay format, how I could use it in the same way I used poetry in my first two books. In my return letter to Monika I had many questions: do you think that the influence movies have had on writing has made today's novel too dialogue-driven? Is the published screenplay the «new fiction»? What if people only read the book after they saw the movie? And if so, could you estimate the degree of frustration experienced by the one million Americans who tried to read *Naked Lunch* after seeing the film? I concluded with a gushing thanks, once again wishing her the best of luck on the project. In my PS I listed the address of the League of Cana-
ᶜ˙˙ⁿ Poets, adding that I knew of at least one or two writers there that might be of interest to her re: the screenplay. And, finally, in my first

PPS in twenty five years, I wrote, in big block letters: WRITE BACK SOON!

I spent the next three weeks immersed in film books. I read screenplays by the Coens, a book on screenwriting by Syd Field, a history of film by Parker Tyler, feminist film theory by Laura Mulvey – everything and anything I could get my hands on – all the while eager to hear back from Monika, eager to hear more about her thoughts on writing and filmmaking. But as the weeks turned into months I began to have my doubts that I would ever hear from Monika again. Maybe she thought I was just some flake who didn't ask the right questions? Or maybe she'd found someone else to write her screenplay and didn't have time for me anymore? I didn't know. So, to get my mind off of Monika's snub, I went out and rented a bunch of movies, stuff that kept coming up in my readings. This didn't help, either. Within a couple of weeks it got to the point where I was watching up to eight movies a day. Then, after one particular day, when I watched *Zabriskie Point*, then *Carnal Knowledge*, then *Killing of a Chinese Bookie*, then *Z*, then *The Sergeant*, then *Bad Timing: A Sensual Obsession*, then *Putney Swope*, then *The Conversation*, then *The Lair of the White Worm*, then *The Player*, I lost it. I spent the next six days in bed, awash in a horrific montage sequence made up of the one-hundred-and-twenty-odd movies I'd seen since I went on my spree (the lowlight being a hallucinatory visit by my mother, played by Art Garfunkel). But on the seventh day my girlfriend, Judy, called upstairs to say a parcel had arrived. It was from Monika.

The parcel was basically a gigantic scrapbook: on one side of the page was Monika's letter; on the other side, a series of articles on screenwriting and filmmaking to which her letter made reference. I spent the next week reading up on everything from Eisenstein's *Strike* to the development of the USSR State Committee on Cinematography, from the unorthodoxy of Tenghiz Abuladze to the ascendancy of the Hungarian pornography industry. And it was fascinating because of what the document said about the particulars of filmmaking in Eastern Europe – no, what dazzled me most about this package was the manner with which it was constructed: Monika's elliptical (and very personal) writing on the backs of these stiff, theoretical texts. It was *so* inspiring. The loose weave of Monika's lyric prose wandering like a drunk from article to article. A sip here, a glass there. A hyphen here, a genre there. So imagine my delight when I came to her PS: she still hadn't found a screenwriter for the project; and then her PPS, where she asked me once again if I would consider writing the screenplay to *A Bunch of Americans Talking*. This time I said yes. It was a conditional yes, but a yes all the same.

In my return letter I mentioned that my main concern stemmed from a conversation Monika and I had during our first meeting, in Berlin, on the eve of the 1995 Berlin Film Festival. Bruce McDonald, who had just optioned my book *Hard Core Logo*, and who had introduced me to Monika, had taken us to an editing suite to see a rough-cut of some off-beat, character-driven film that a friend of his was working on (I can't remember what it was called, but it was okay). During the walk back to Monika's hotel the topic turned to actor improvisation. Although Monika and I both agreed on the importance of actor improvisation, we disagreed on the extent of that improvisation. Bruce mentioned some of John Cassavetes' earlier films — *Shadows, Faces, Husbands* — and asked us how we liked them. Well, I *love* those films. And I love the fact that they were brought about through intense actor workshopping. But Monika didn't think much of them. She said she liked their intensity — but complained they were too hysterical, too meandering, too indulgent. I told her that these were the very qualities I liked about Cassavetes' films. And I told her how, if I was to ever make films one day, I would most certainly look to Cassavetes as a model; that I admired his relationship with his actors, his crazy use of sound, his unwavering support for independent filmmaking. Then a funny thing happened: Monika began to describe a scene in *Shadows*, a scene she really liked, but a scene that neither Bruce nor I remembered. Bruce asked her if perhaps she was talking about a different film. Monika then gave a quick summary of a film that wasn't *Shadows* at all. In fact, as it turned out, Monika had never seen a film by John Cassavetes.

Anyway, we all had a good laugh over it, and Monika promised that she would try to catch up with those films one day. But the moment kinda stuck. And the question remained: if Monika had never seen a Cassavetes film, how is it that her complaint about those films seemed so consistent with the many people who had seen his films and didn't like them? And if I was now going to be involved in a film with Monika, wouldn't I want to be assured that we were on the same page, so to speak, as far as the kind of film we were going to make? Especially a film that seemed as chatty and character-driven as the title *A Bunch of Americans Talking* suggested? And especially since I had never actually seen a film by Monika Herendy?

It was a small detail. And it was made that much smaller with Monika's next letter. In it she wrote of her embarrassment that night in Berlin, how immediately after the festival she set out to watch not only all of John Cassavetes' films but all of Robert Altman's films as well. And she apologized relentlessly for what she called her « Soviet conditioning »: how when she started out as a filmmaker, in the 1980s, in Leningrad, she was forced into membership with the propagandistic Goskino (The USSR State Committee on Cinematography), and how that experience, she felt, not so much compromised the string of embarrassing « patriot » films that appeared under her « direction » but legislated against the kind of creativity one might find in the films of, say, a John Cassavetes or a Robert Altman. But she also wrote of how excited she was that I would be willing to write the screenplay for *A Bunch of Americans Talking*: how this would be an opportunity for her to get back to her filmmaking instincts, and how this project could lend itself to some of the very things we now seemed to share in the films of John Cassavetes and Robert Altman. The rest of Monika's letter was made up of details regarding the conversations she hoped would provide the basis for the screenplay, and how that screenplay would provide the basis for the actor workshops. My task, then, was to both shape these conversations and create an environment in which they might take place – which was fine by me. Also fine by me was the contract stapled to the back of the letter – and the decent advance upon signing. I returned the signed contract the next day (along with my email address) and sat down to work.

What happened next was long and involved. The short form goes like this.

About a month after returning the contract (and about seventy pages into the screenplay) I began receiving emails from Monika on a daily basis. At first the email messages were helpful: Could we add this kind of character to that kind of conversation? Could we make this kind of character less sexy and that kind of character more violent? Could we make one of the conversations contingent upon another conversation, while, at the same time, make some conversations oblivious to others? Simple stuff, slight alterations to the original character sketches – a snip here, a patch there. But with each passing day the mail began to get more and more erratic. For example, one morning I checked my box and all it said was «That handsome man from *Baywatch*. Think about it.» Okay, I thought, I'm open to cryptic suggestions. But then the next day (Remembrance Day, as I recall) I received another note from Monika: a simple hello-how-are-you? kinda thing; but attached to the note was a document written in this weird ransom font, and all it said was «Whatever I'm saying yesterday was not what I've said today.» That's when I started to get worried. I was closing in on a first draft, so I emailed Monika and asked whether these one-liners of hers were her way of asking to see something of the screenplay. (After all, the only thing I'd sent her thus far was a very rough treatment – which she'd liked.) A couple of hours later she emailed back. But she didn't answer my question. Instead, she provided a new list of suggestions: Could we cut back on the class analysis? Could we stretch the sex talk out even further? Could we make those characters who would be most likely of our sympathy the least sympathetic? I mean – yes, I was concerned about overstating the class analysis. And, no, I didn't want to stretch the sex talk out any further. And, well, maybe I was representing those characters most likely of our sympathy as too sympathetic. Hell, I didn't know. Is this what collaboration was all about? *I mean – you're the one who seems to know what's going on better than I do, Monika. Why don't I just send you the fucking thing?* So I emailed Monika, asking her again if she wanted to see the screenplay. And again, a few hours later, a response. But this time it wasn't from Monika. It was from Klaus 9.

What little I knew of Klaus 9 I knew from Bruce. I knew he was a rich German eccentric who travelled the world in a private jet and paid people to throw parties for him, and that he was associated in some way with Monika (whether as a producer or an investor I wasn't sure); but he was a reliable guy in the business sense, and a great supporter of Monika's films. So I wasn't entirely surprised to hear from him. (In fact, it was quite fortuitous that I did hear from Klaus 9 because I had yet to receive my advance money and he was, as it turned out, going to be producing this picture.) Anyway, I welcomed Klaus 9's email. He recognized my frustration and had some calming words. He also told me how Monika was under a great deal of pressure at the moment (which, perhaps, explained some of the more cryptic suggestions she'd sent me), and that she had just left for the Black Sea, where she was going to be shooting a series of ads for one of his companies, but that she would like to see a first draft when she got back in two weeks. Klaus 9 said that I should be receiving a cheque in the mail the next day for both the advance and the completed first draft, and that he was sorry that I hadn't received my advance on time (which, as he mentioned earlier, was probably owing to Monika's fragile emotional state).

Sure enough, the cheque arrived the next day. This was a great relief, because not only was I broke but I was also beginning to have serious doubts about whether or not this project was ever going to happen. Relieved of my poverty (and my misgivings), I spent the next two weeks trying to finish the first draft of *A Bunch of Americans Talking*. I say *trying* because screenwriting was turning out to be a much harder job than I expected. But my time was up, and I had to send something. So what I sent was a long note to Monika explaining the problems I was having with the weave, and that if I had a little more time I could at least send her something I could live with. A couple of hours later I received a very compassionate email from Monika telling me that I shouldn't be so precious about the first draft; that this was, after all, a collaborative medium, and her input was essential to the collaboration; and that, once again, this screenplay was only going to be a rough guide anyway – the particulars of which the actors were going to « narrativize » in the workshops. My fears unallayed, I quickly emailed Monika asking for just three more days. She responded just as quickly with a counter-offer of two, noting that if I were to check page six of our agreement (which I never really looked at in the first place) I would notice that I was already a week overdue and in serious breach of contract. Bugged about the breach, I spent the next forty-eight hours bent over the laptop, pasting together what Monika overheard that week in Cannes two years before with what amounted to over five hundred suggestions to a text she had not yet seen but hopefully could well imagine – the screenplay to what I was now calling *American Whiskey Bar*.

With great reluctance (and, looking back, with great regret), I emailed Monika that first draft of *American Whiskey Bar*. What else could I do? I was under contract. And it's my own fault for not reading the details of the agreement in the first place. Still, I know that if I just had a little more time I could've shaped it into something halfway decent, something I wouldn't be so horribly ashamed of. But then again, to what end? The script had always been intended as an annotated map for Monika and the actors to negotiate a story. Who knows what they would have come up? I mean – that was the idea, right? They were supposed to take it somewhere, let loose with it, tighten it up. I kept up my end of things: I pasted the conversations and the characters together; I came up with the setting. I did my bit. It wasn't my fault things didn't turn out on Monika's end. But that just brings me back to the beginning: if I'd delivered a better script then I wouldn't be feeling so shitty. At least I'd be able to say that the script I submitted was well-written.

So what happened? Well, to be honest, I'm not totally sure. What I am sure of, though, is that the film was made – BUT IT WAS MADE EXACTLY AS I HAD WRITTEN IT! Not one word changed, not one word added or subtracted! Hence my embarrassment. Hence my shame at having written a piece that was meant as a basis for improvisation, only to have it performed verbatim.

Now, I imagine you must have many questions. Well, so do I. For I have gone insane trying to come to terms with what's happened. But rather than go into detail here I'll just let Monika explain it to you in her «Introduction,» because the purpose of my «Preface» isn't to speculate on what happens once a script is in the hands of a filmmaker but a chance to give you a bit of background on how the screenplay came to be written and, most importantly, why I have chosen to publish it.

Why have I chosen to publish the screenplay to *American Whiskey Bar?* Why have I chosen to publish a work of such profound embarrassment? A work that I am truly ashamed to have my name attached? A work whose mere mention brings a burning sensation to my ears? A work that makes me want to bury my head in my mother's lap and cry?

I am publishing *American Whiskey Bar* because – and I know this sounds silly – I want to stop the madness. Believe me, a day does not go by where I don't get a phone call or a piece of mail or bump into someone who has heard about *American Whiskey Bar* and wants to know what it's about or why I wrote it or how they heard about it from a friend (or a friend-of-a-friend) who thought it was either the most provocative film they've ever seen or the worst piece of crap they've ever had to sit through. So enough's enough! I am sick to death of hearing about something that is so different from the film I was involved with as to constitute an entirely new project. I'm tired of the fuss, the buzz, and the bother – the ridiculously mythic proportions the film *American Whiskey Bar* has taken on. I mean, it's gotten to the point where my abilities as a writer are surpassed only by my reputation as a writer of work I am completely unaware of. But it's more than that: not only am I tired of having to explain a work I have no interest in but I'm also tired of lying about it. Oh, I denied it at first. I told people it was just a rumour, that there was no *American Whiskey Bar,* or that another Michael Turner wrote it. And then I went the flippant route and told people it was a sham, that I only did it for the money. But it wouldn't stop. And since there is no chance that any of you who are reading this are ever going to see this movie (as you'll probably find out why in Milena's «Afterword»), I have no choice but to set the record straight: to publish once and for all the screenplay to the film that all of you are so curious about, the film that has caused me so much grief.

Michael Turner

VANCOUVER, 1997

Introduction

LET ME SAY at the outset that I only agreed to write the «Introduction» to *American Whiskey Bar* on the condition that I be allowed an unadulterated response to Michael's «Preface.» I knew Michael was upset with what happened with the film – and I pretty much knew what he was going to say about it. But there were a lot of things that happened during the film's production that Michael was unaware of – which is why it is imperative that I be given a chance to respond to Michael's complaints, and, thus, hopefully provide a proper context for what really went wrong during the making of *American Whiskey Bar*.

First of all, Michael's remembrance of our first meeting differs somewhat from mine. Yes, it is true that we were introduced to each other by Bruce McDonald. And yes, it is true that Bruce took us to see some stupid movie about a bunch of Irish teenagers. But no, it wasn't the films of John Cassavetes that we talked about afterwards – it was the films of Robert Altman. A small detail, to be sure, but a relevant one. Yet a detail nowhere near as relevant as the one Michael neglected to mention: after the three of us returned to my suite for drinks it was Michael who first brought up the idea of writing for film – not me. This is not to imply, however, that I wasn't interested in what he had to say or that I discouraged him from the topic or that I didn't pursue him as avidly as I did when it came time to find a screenwriter for what I was originally calling *A Bunch of Americans Talking*. On the contrary, I welcomed his enthusiasm with open arms. I had wanted to meet Michael ever since Bruce gave me a copy of *Hard Core Logo*, a book I loved not so much for its story (which is age-old) but for its construction. *Hard Core Logo* has a visual sensibility, a cinematic quality that suggests it could have been written as much with a channel-changer as a pen and paper. (In fact, when Bruce told me he was going to be making a movie based on *Hard Core Logo* I was shocked: « But, Bruce,» I said, « the book *is* a movie. It's a movie with pages.») Anyway, like I said, it was Michael who first raised the topic of writing for film – not me. So I think it's important that I address this issue right away, because I feel that Michael's sense of hurt over this project has led him to recreate the story of our first meeting (indeed, of our whole relationship) as a matter of self-preservation.

Another thing Michael neglected to mention (which also stems from our first meeting) were the details of the Cannes conversations. These conversations were important to me in that I had never heard Americans talk to each other before. (Let me qualify that: I had met Americans and I had hung out with Americans – but it wasn't until Cannes that I actually heard them speaking to each other.) Also, it wasn't until Cannes that the English language began to make sense to me. That's why the moment was so significant. As a teenager growing up in Eastern Europe in the 1970s, I harboured an intense curiosity about America. America seemed so wild, so excessive, so sexy – the very things that were put down under Soviet rule. But now, with the way the world has changed in the last few years, with the so-called «opening up» of Eastern Europe, I have become scared of what America is capable of. And I don't mean scared in the nuclear obliteration sense. No, it's more the opposite: I am scared of the insidiousness, the ideological, the infective potential that is America – and how the very things that once seemed so sunny about America now cloud me. This is what I was trying to get at with *American Whiskey Bar*. And it was on that night, in Berlin, that I first told Michael and Bruce the details of those conversations.

And it was Michael who seemed so especially interested. And although it was Bruce who happened to suggest that I make a movie about those conversations, it was me who decided to send Michael a letter asking him to write it.

So what did I hear at Cannes? Well, I heard a lot of things. Ambition and greed, desire and lust, compassion and patronage, regret and regression, emphasis and exaggeration, lies and expediencies – all of it, at once, swirling around me, strobic, a raving humanity. And how did I feel about it? Strangely narcissistic. The narcissism that comes with the moment of discovery (which, in this instance, was finding myself capable of a language only seconds before coming to terms with what was actually being said). Indeed, the beauty of discovering that which informs you, reaffirms you – then the horror that strikes once you've realized that it's ugly. The horror that is finding yourself blindfolded and covered with glue as you're being led into a gigantic rat's nest, as you slowly become aware, with each passing step, of the weight you're taking on. Of course, how I felt about what I heard at Cannes that week differed wildly from what I told Michael that night in Berlin; for my story was basic: a few character sketches, some conversation topics, descriptions. Nevertheless, I must have made quite a strong impression on Michael, because, judging from his first outline (and the only thing I have seen of *American Whiskey Bar* thus far), his initial rendering of the Cannes conversations was remarkably spot on.

Another matter that I must take issue with is the correspondence between Michael and myself. Although I enjoyed our early letters (especially his use of a device then unknown to me, the PS) I must protest his depiction of me as a beggar; that I begged him to write the screenplay for what was then known as *A Bunch of Americans Talking*. I think this characterization is both erroneous and unfair. Yes, I was very interested in having Michael write the screenplay – but no, I did not beg him to write it. Again, as I mentioned earlier, I feel it is out of a sense of hurt that Michael has chosen to be so creative in his retelling of our relationship. Yet, given the circumstances surrounding the making of

American Whiskey Bar, I can forgive him this. However, what desperately needs clarifying (and this is no fault of Michael's) concerns our email correspondence – specifically that which Michael referred to as my «cryptic suggestions.» I did not write those. Those were not written by me. The person who wrote that shit is evil. He is, without question, the cruelest person in the world, the scourge of the earth. He is the man who has forever ruined not only my life but my art. A man whose name alone is so hurtful to me that my hand refuses to make its shape. A name that I have had to ask Michael's publisher to insert into this «Introduction» upon receipt of the text – Klaus 9.

Now, before going any further, I must step back and tell you where I've come from. For what I'm about to tell you is very difficult for me – these are things that not even Michael knows – but they are essential if you are going to understand what happened during the making of *American Whiskey Bar.* I will try to be as brief as possible. But please, hear me out.

Michael mentioned in his «Preface» that I was trained in the Soviet Union. This is true. I left Hungary at the age of seventeen to study filmmaking in Leningrad, with the hope of one day making films. Unfortunately my timing was bad; I came to Russia during the 1980s, when young filmmakers were becoming less inclined towards experimentation and more concerned with state funding. One of the assumptions was that young filmmakers (if they wanted to make films) must seek favour from the Goskino (which, for you in Canada, would be the Soviet equivalent to Telefilm). Approval from the Goskino meant not just making films but making films that reaffirmed the singularity of the communist way of life – a life that, at that time (despite what you may have seen on TV), was becoming more and more oppressive. Not so much in terms of economic oppression, but in oppression of free-thought. Nevertheless, I carried on. I directed three feature-length films between 1983 and 1987, none of which I am particularly proud. However, with the so-called «opening up» of Eastern Europe, I found myself doing more and more work outside the state. And the kind of work I found myself doing was pornography.

How one gets involved in making pornographic films is not so cut-and-dry. Often it is something that you just wake up one day and realize you are doing (rather than waking up one day and deciding to do). In my case, I was trying to raise money for a documentary I wanted to make about Bulgarian prostitutes working along the Black Sea. I had travelled to the 1990 Venice Film Festival, where I was to meet some Cuban businessmen whom I'd first met during a Russian-Cuban co-production a few years before. It was there that I met Klaus 9.

The meeting with the Cuban businessmen never happened. I was stood up. And I was broke, too. I put everything I had on that bus trip to Venice. It was a gamble, and I lost. So there I was, wandering around the festival, walking past line-ups to movies I would never see, wondering how I was ever going to get home, when I met him. It was at that moment a most violent wave of hunger set in (I hadn't eaten in two days) and I found myself staring at a large group of what those in America call «beautiful people» — eight or nine of them sitting around a tiny white table outside a café. And on that table was a circle of dirty glasses. And inside that circle was a half-eaten bun. And I wanted it — I wanted that bun. Just then I heard someone call my name. I was so preoccupied with my hunger I didn't know where it was coming from. I found myself spinning around, looking up and down, delirious. Then I heard it again. It was coming from the table with the bun. It was Evgeny, my old chum from film school.

When I came to, I was being carried over to the table. I could hear them talking about me, reviewing my career, listing off the films they liked — or didn't. One gruff voice wondered what had become of me. Another voice presumed I had gone off to America to make pornos. Yet another voice, a woman's, said, «Oh, Monika Herendy. I thought she was dead.» Then this sort of fey-sounding man said, «She is, darling. Just nobody noticed.» And then there was laughter. And it was awful. And I hated it. It was like the worst part of my life passing before me — but just the audio portion. And that's when I met him. That fat ass.

Klaus. He was holding out the chair Evgeny was sitting me down on. He offered me a glass of water, then called out to a waiter to bring me some pasta. I stared at him as I drank the lemony water, thanking him with my eyes, trying to remember where I might have seen him before. He introduced himself. « My name is Klaus 9. We met once before, at a theatre school in Dresden. You were casting, I was acting. But you wouldn't remember me.» It was true. I didn't.

Thus began my long employment with Klaus 9. For the next six years I was in charge of making his fetish films. It worked like this: I'd sit at home and wait for the phone to ring. Then the phone would ring. If it was Klaus, I'd write down everything he said about what time I was supposed to be at the airport and what he wanted me to do once I'd flown to wherever it was he wanted me to be. I'd hang up the phone, grab my overnight bag (which I always kept packed for those moments), and go downstairs and hail a taxi. I'd take the taxi to the airport, pick up my ticket, look at it to find out what part of the world I'd be flying to, then get on the plane. Once I'd arrived, I'd be met by whomever it was that Klaus had sent to get me. I'd go with that person to a hotel, where I'd meet with my director of photography, my old school chum, Evgeny. We'd discuss Klaus' notes, then call for our escort. He or she would take us to a large suite where we'd meet with whomever it was that Klaus had assembled for a cast. Then we'd check to see if we had all the right props. Anything we didn't have we'd send the escort to get. Then we'd start shooting. And we wouldn't stop until we finished. When we finished, Evgeny would take the film and leave. About a week later Evgeny would show up at my door and we'd go across town to edit. Once the film was edited, Evgeny and I would go out for dinner and get drunk and talk about how this would be the last time we'd ever work for Klaus 9 again, and how the next time we worked together, it would be on one of our own films. Then I'd say goodbye to Evgeny, and he and the film would disappear in a taxi. Then I'd get into my taxi and disappear back to my apartment, where I'd lie in bed all night thinking about Evgeny telling Klaus everything about our conversation at dinner. And then I'd cry. And then I'd fall asleep.

But *American Whiskey Bar* was supposed to change all that. *American Whiskey Bar* was supposed to be my ticket to respectability, a chance for me to get reacquainted with my art, to meet new people like Michael Turner. But this was not the case. In fact, everything that *American Whiskey Bar* was supposed to be became the opposite. It is the classic story of one-step-forward-two-steps-back. For *American Whiskey Bar* has forever ruined me as a filmmaker. This is what happened.

Once Michael agreed to write the screenplay I was ecstatic. But it wasn't easy. It was like shoeing donkeys trying to get him to commit. However, once we cleared up our misunderstanding over what «improvise» meant (my English was quite rusty back then, and I kept thinking he was saying the word «prophesize»), Michael was in. Which was perfect timing because in the two months it was going to take him to write the first draft I would have finally saved up enough money to shoot what was still known as *A Bunch of Americans Talking*. Oh, and I had it all planned out, too! I knew these terrific actors from Bratislava who spoke excellent English and were into doing the kind of weird stuff I was hoping Michael would get up to. Plus I had an excellent film crew lined up here in Budapest. The only problem was getting access to a good camera, and the only person I knew with a good camera was Evgeny. But as much as I loved Evgeny, I couldn't trust him. Evgeny was in way too deep with Klaus. But then a miracle happened. About a month after Michael agreed to write the screenplay, Evgeny showed up on my door step — with camera in tow. He had just been fired by Klaus.

Evgeny was distraught. He told me the two of them had had a terrible blow-out in St Petersburg. I asked him what it was about, and he told me it was about us. Apparently Klaus had demanded to know what we talked about at dinner after our last editing session. But this time Evgeny, who had always been so weak, who had always told Klaus everything, refused. Evgeny said Klaus flew into a rage, that he threw his drink in Evgeny's face and started slapping him around. In public. In front of all of Evgeny's friends. Evgeny then told Klaus that he'd had enough, that he wasn't going to take it anymore. That's when Klaus picked up a beer bottle and smashed it over Evgeny's head. Evgeny took his cap off and tipped his head toward me, insisting that I touch his matted crown. I told him it was okay, that I was very sorry for what had happened, but I didn't need to touch his wound. I believed him.

I asked Evgeny what he was going to do. He shrugged, then looked away. He said he had a couple of ideas for some films, but he didn't have any money saved. I looked over at his camera, then looked back at him. He was looking at me. Then he looked over at his camera and told me he'd probably have to sell it. I told him that was ridiculous, that he was a filmmaker, an artist.... But he cut me off. He told me that maybe it was time for a change, that maybe he should just sell his camera and go to America, start over, maybe work in the porno industry over there. I looked over at his camera again. When I looked back he was crying. He told me he was scared, that he felt lost. Then I started crying, too. And as he babbled on, all I could think about was how much he helped me back when we were students in Leningrad; how I was just an idiot kid from Budapest who had bad clothes and barely spoke Russian; how Evgeny befriended me and helped me learn the language and intro-duced me to people and, as much as I hated to say it, rescued me that day in Venice. So that's when I told him my plan.

We stayed up all night chatting. The more I told him about *A Bunch of Americans Talking*, the more he seemed to perk up. In fact, he loved the idea. He thought it would make an excellent picture. And he wanted desperately to be a part of it. And I desperately wanted him to be a part of it, too. He wanted to know when we could start. I told him that Michael wouldn't have a script ready for at least another month, but by that time I would have saved up enough money to pay for the screenplay and begin pre-production. But I had everything else budgeted – crew, film, talent, editing. All I needed was one more gig with Klaus. And if that happened in the next couple of weeks (which seemed likely, since it had been a while since we'd last done something) then I could quit and begin right away. Evgeny told me that Klaus had just rented a spa down south, on the

Black Sea, and that he had a bunch of new groupies hanging around, so maybe he was close to setting something up. I reminded Evgeny that because Klaus was now without a cameraman he might not be as close to production as we think. Evgeny smiled, then brushed off the suggestion. He said guys like him were a dime a dozen.

Sure enough, Evgeny was right. The next day the phone rang. It was Klaus. He told me the usual things and I dutifully wrote them down. Before leaving I briefed Evgeny on the project thus far, giving him my director notes, as well as the treatment that Michael emailed a couple of weeks before. I also gave him Michael's email address and encouraged Evgeny to introduce himself, since Michael, at that point, had an interesting idea about camera placement, suggesting that we set up a stationary camera in the middle of four tables and pan from scene to scene. Evgeny seemed excited by this idea and promised me that he would most certainly get in touch with Michael. Then he walked me down the stairs to my taxi, gave me a big hug, and wished me the best of luck, insisting that if Klaus gave me any trouble to just bear with it, because, as he put it: « Once you're finished with this gig, we're finished with Klaus forever.» Then we said our goodbyes – forever.

I should have known something was up when I got to the airport and looked at my ticket. Bulgaria, it said. Varna, Bulgaria. But I could only laugh by then. I was too giddy. Bulgaria! Of course! Was it not Bulgaria that took me to Venice years before, where I first met Klaus 9? And now I would finally be going back to Bulgaria to shoot one of his stupid fetish films, with his stupid hanger-on prostitutes. It seemed so perfectly ironic. And the more I kept thinking about it, the more I felt bolstered by the irony. Fucking Bulgaria! I kept saying to myself, changing planes in Sofia. Fucking Varna, I kept saying to myself, as I got off the plane and met my escort. A fucking documentary on Bulgarian prostitutes, I kept saying to myself as we pulled up to the spa, where Klaus 9 was waiting.

I knew something was up. Klaus was never on location. He always said it defeated the purpose. («Where's my surprise?» he would say. « How could I get an erection if I saw how one of my little films was made?») I was quick to reminded him of this. «What the fuck are you doing here?» I demanded, hoping a belligerent tone would somehow mask the fear that was clogging my throat. One of his assistants stepped forward. She told me that Klaus had seen a documentary on Hitchcock and had «discovered direction,» and that from now on I would be taking Evgeny's place on camera. Klaus then pushed the assistant aside, then gave me his own answer, a very strange one, an answer that would only make sense to me some time later: «You know, Monika,» he said, putting a fat hand on my shoulder, «maybe if you didn't actually direct the movies you made you might enjoy them a little more.» Then he laughed. And as he laughed he looked to his crew, tossing his fat laugh around the room like a boulder, laughing at them until they all laughed back. I felt my ears burn, my eyes welled up. But then I grabbed onto Evgeny's parting words, how «once [I was] finished with this gig, we were finished with Klaus forever.» And I took comfort in those words. I kept repeating them over and over in my head until, all of a sudden, I felt them slip away. I began to hear what Evgeny said before that: how if Klaus were to give me any trouble to just bear with it, because....

Evgeny knew all along. He knew that Klaus would be there. But how did he know? He knew because Klaus told him. Just as Klaus told him to tell me that Klaus had beaten him up, fired him. Just as Klaus had told him to find out what I was up to. Just as Evgeny *did* find out what I was up to. And now Evgeny was in my apartment, with my notes, with Michael's email address. And I was in Bulgaria. And I was standing before Klaus. His huge, shitty laugh. His arm waving at the first AD, beckoning him to bring out the talent: the African man in the lab coat, the two prim and proper women – parodies of the women I had interviewed for my proposed documentary, the one I went to Venice for. But how could this be happening? How could this have happened?

The Bulgarian film was made, of course. And naturally it was nowhere near the documentary I had originally planned on making. It was a standard Klaus 9 fetish film. The African man in the lab coat is the doctor. The older prim and proper woman is the nurse. The younger

woman is the patient. She has come to see the doctor about an undis-
closed fear. The doctor has an unusual medical practice. Et cetera. The
whole thing a 180-degree flip from my documentary. And Klaus knew
it. His Bulgarian film was meant to humiliate me. And humiliate me he
did. Initially he found this very amusing, as he knew he would, keeping
a video camera on me the whole time – hoping to catch every wince,
every tear, every breakdown he felt I was capable of. But I gave him
nothing. And the more I gave him nothing, the angrier he became. And
the angrier he became, the closer I came to salvaging some self-respect.
But I had no idea what was to come of this. And, looking back, it's
amazing I didn't, for if I had I may very well have lost my nerve.

It was the last day of filming, after twenty-one days in a Bulgarian
spa, and we were in the middle of the final scene. The African actor
playing the doctor, who had been worked like a horse by Klaus from
day one, was having problems maintaining an erection. Klaus, who by
this time was already purple with rage over my failure to behave miser-
ably as he expected, was screaming at the young actor, taunting him,
calling him all sorts of things, which I could clearly see (from my
close-up camera position) was having the opposite effect on the
problem at hand. The African actor (who I must say had performed
tirelessly up to this point) finally asked if it were possible for the
younger actor he was doing the scene with (who had small patches of
eczema on her palms) could apply some cream to her hands, as their
dryness was chafing his penis. Klaus called for the script. After a short
consultation with the first AD Klaus decided we had enough master
shots, and that we would be doing close-ups – with a hand-double.
Then he looked at me.

The first thing that went through my head was no. (And I think this
showed on my face, for the video camera that had been documenting
my every move was now zooming in.) Klaus was moving towards me.
He came right up to me and pushed me off my mount. I lay there
stunned as he took aim through the close-up camera. The first AD then
grabbed my wrist and pulled me up, sitting me at the foot of the

camera, positioning my wrist in front of the lens. Klaus was giggling. I could hear one of the crew say that this was the happiest they'd seen him since we started production. The next thing I know, the camera's rolling. The first AD's letting go of my wrist, my arm was floating there. I looked at it. Then I saw the second AD leading the African actor towards me. The second AD opened my hand and laid the actor's penis across my palm. Then he closed my hand. I looked over at the documentary camera and saw my blank expression reflected in the lens. Then I felt a hand clasp my elbow as my arm began to shake. I looked over to see the first AD, the one who was doing the shaking. I could feel my hand begin to swell, I began to feel myself losing my grip. Klaus yelled for me to watch the action, that I was losing the field. I looked at the action: a hand travelling up and down a stiffening penis. Just then a drop of water landed on the hand. I looked up at the actor's tight sweaty face, his clenched teeth, then back at the hand and the penis. The hand was now moving faster. The penis and the hand looked like one thing, melded together. I stopped my hand and squeezed, pulling the penis down 90 degrees as it erupted into the lens. The focus-pull screamed.

That's when Klaus lost it. He jumped from the camera and began to beat me. Not just slapping me around, but really laying into me. Yet all I could feel was my hand, still in its fist, punching back. That's the last I thing I remember.

The next thing I knew, I was coming to in the hospital, still in Varna. I had been in and out of coma for the past two months. The doctor told me I was lucky to be alive, that when I was brought in I looked like a side of raw beef. One of the nurses told me I should be thankful to have been in a coma, that the coma gave my wounds time to heal, and that if I hadn't been in a coma for so long, I wouldn't have been able to stand the sight of myself. When I asked how I wound up in the hospital in the first place, they told me I was brought in by some garbagemen who found me in an alley near the beach.

A couple of weeks later, while checking out, I asked the administrator how much I owed. She told me everything had been taken care of. The administrator smiled, then said something about how there are still guardian angels at work in this world, selfless people who do good unto others without so much as leaving a forwarding address. I asked the administrator if the hospital would have taken me in if there had been nobody to pick up the tab. The administrator made a play-shameful face and said no, she was sorry, she didn't think they would have, that when they brought me into the hospital two months ago everybody thought I was just some Black Sea prostitute.

But I digress. I mean, I could go on. I could tell you how I spent another two months in physiotherapy, and another month in psycho-therapy, only to return home to find my apartment rented to someone else, all my personal possessions disposed of. But why bother? You've read this far only because you want to know about *American Whiskey Bar*, right?

American Whiskey Bar was shot and edited in January and February of 1997. Although my name appears on the director credit, everyone knows the film was made by the film's producer, Klaus 9, while I lay comatose in a Bulgarian hospital. Everyone knows the film was shot by the brilliant Evgeny Churkin, a month before his body was found floating in the Oder – just as they know the reason I was in Bulgaria in the first place was because I was working as a Black Sea prostitute. As well, everyone knows the film was written by Michael Turner, based on conversations overheard by filmmaker Bruce McDonald at the 1995 Berlin Film Festival – just as they know I gave up filmmaking because I was upset with the dissolution of the Soviet Bloc and the end of my filmmaking career as a Russian lackey. And, finally, as everyone knows, the has-been Hollywood studio actors that Klaus 9 so brilliantly «redis-covered,» who apparently recited their lines so convincingly in *American Whiskey Bar,* have (so I hear) rocketed back to the top of the thespian money heap – just as I have found myself picking up radio transmissions broadcasting their good fortune in the steel plate that lies beneath my scalp.

So, I appreciate this opportunity, Michael, to provide you with an «Introduction» to the *American Whiskey Bar* screenplay. I hope I haven't been *too* digressive in my attempt to let you in on how this film was «made.» Naturally, I regret that we were unable to see it through the way we originally envisioned. Perhaps sometime down the road we may get a chance to work together on something else, something more along the lines of what we talked about earlier? A real collaboration, though. Not like what really happened with *American Whiskey Bar*. In the meantime, I look forward to finally reading the screenplay to the film I am said to have made – and that you most certainly wrote.

Monika Herendy
BUDAPEST, 1997

ps *I have sent along some rather blurred images that I downloaded off the Web – photographs that were allegedly taken (covertly) by a C. Rossi, a make-up artist on the* American Whiskey Bar *set. I would have included the Web address, but the site came and went within a couple of weeks.*

26

American Whiskey Bar

DRAMATIS PERSONÆ

A	sanitation worker
B	sanitation worker
C	sanitation worker
P	film guy
Q	film guy
HE	law clerk
SHE	law clerk
HER BROTHER	salesman
RAMÒN	boxer
WOMAN 1	legal secretary
WOMAN 2	legal secretary

AFRICAN EXCHANGE STUDENT /
LIBERIAN/SAO BOSA

POLICEMAN 1

POLICEMAN 2

THE BARTENDER

INT. A DIMLY LIT BAR — LATE-AFTERNOON FRIDAY.

Right away we get the feeling that this establishment was built in the early 1960s, a place where Jack Lemmon's character may have had an after-work drink before returning home to The Apartment. *However, as we move about the room, we see how the joint wears its changes, the passing of each decade, its '60s polish lost.*

To the far-left is a long narrow bar. It is empty — except for THE BARTENDER. THE BARTENDER, *an old man (60s) in a starched white shirt and black tie, is washing out a beer glass. Behind him is a bottle shelf set against a huge mirror. The size of the shelf suggests that it was originally built to accommodate a variety of liquors, but now the gaps between bottles are filled with framed 8 × 10 photos (*JFK *and Jackie, Muhammad Ali knocking out Sonny Liston), newspaper clippings (the shooting of Martin Luther King, the Apollo moon landing, the American withdrawal from Vietnam), sports memorabilia (a worn grey tennis ball signed by Bobby Riggs, a souvenir pennant from the Team* USA *Olympic hockey team), and assorted trinkets (a Bicentennial toothpick-holder, a Walter Mondale campaign button, a postcard of the Space Shuttle, a ticket stub from the premiere of the movie* Wall Street, *an Operation Desert Storm coffee cup, etc.)*

To the far-right of the bar, in the foreground, we see a square area set aside for tables and chairs. This area is also empty. Beyond the tables and chairs we see the walls, the distressed wainscoting, the unfinished strips of wood where booths might have been. And we see a similar thing above the wainscoting: the fresh squares where lit paintings once hung. These paintings have been replaced with the twisted neon that is beer promotion.

Enter three sanitation workers. White. They are dressed in white coveralls. A is a gruff crew boss (50). B is an energetic kid (early 20s)s. And C is a slow-moving, cynical guy (mid-30s). They exchange hellos with the bartender and pull up chairs around a small table closest to the bar: A in the middle, B camera-right, C camera-left. The bartender brings them three Buds. The kid begins the pitch.

B

Okay. There's this young couple and they have a baby. Everything's normal about this couple: they're well-adjusted; they have good incomes; they love each other very, very much. And they love their baby very, very much, too. But they've got this problem: their baby won't stop crying. And they're at their wits' end as to what to do about it. They know the baby's crying because it's hungry. But they've tried everything: doctors, formulas – nothing helps. *The baby needs mother's milk.* So they go to a park and kidnap a young welfare mother and *her* baby. The young couple's baby takes to the kidnapped mother's breast no problem. Unfortunately, though, through some household mishap, the kidnapped mother's baby dies. In the ensuing confusion, the kidnapped woman escapes and calls the cops. The young couple are arrested and charged with first-degree murder. A high-profile lawyer comes to the young couple's aid. The lawyer urges them to plead not guilty. He builds a defense on the basis of discrimination: the young couple is a gay male couple.

A

I see Redford as the lawyer.

c *winces.*

> B
>
> What about Sarandon as the kidnapped mother?

> A
>
> No, we need someone younger.

> B
>
> Why not Sarandon? She's a natural! A low-key hysteric.

> A
> *(angrily)*
>
> Forget it! She's too old. What about Demi?

> C
> *(absently)*
>
> Demi won't do dead babies.

> B
>
> What about Laura Dern?

> A
>
> We'll cast the lawyer first.

> C
> *(to* A*)*
>
> You said Redford.

> A
>
> Great. Are we agreed on Redford?

> B
>
> Redford or Warren Oates, yeah.

> A
>
> Hello?

> C
>
> Warren Oates is dead.

B
(surprised)

What?! *When?*

A

A million years ago.

C

Hang on a minute. Whaddaya mean Redford or Warren Oates? How do you end up with those two guys in the same sentence?

B

I don't know. It just came out that way. But yeah – Redford for sure.

C

And what about this couple? How're we gonna do that? The best part of your pitch is not knowing it's a same-sex couple till the middle of the picture.

B

Well, we could do a POV from the couple's perspective.

A

Whaddaya mean a POV from the couple's perspective?! What happens when they look at each other? Are we gonna see another camera?

B

It could be done with one camera.

A

Like what?! Are they Siamese-twin faggots or something?! That's the most stupidest thing I have ever heard in my life.

B

Well, um, if they were a really tight couple like they're supposed to be then, yeah, it might be an interesting conceit.

A

Conceit?!
(raising his fist, à la Ralph Kramden.)
I'll show ya a fuckin' conceit!

C

I've got a gay couple living behind me and they fight all the time.

A *shifts his body to face* C.

A

A couple of gays behind you? I'll bet they're fighting all the time. Probably fighting to get a crack at your lame ass, no doubt.

B *laughs.*

C *makes a «yeah, whatever» face.*

A
(*to* B)

What else ya got?

B

Same thing. But we go with a straight couple.

A

I see Nicolas Cage and...what's-her-name, the chick who played his wife in *Raising Arizona*.

C

Forget it. Cage's too huge. He'd want too much money. Besides, I doubt those two would wanna be teamed up again.

B

No, you're right. We gotta come up with a new couple. How about Keanu and Jennifer Jason Leigh?

C

Too boring. They'd put everyone to sleep.

A

I've changed my mind. I want DeNiro as the lawyer. And I want him to be a fag lawyer. And I want his lover to be that little wop kid from *The Basketball Journals*.

C

Diaries.

A

Whatever. But I want a love scene between those two. And I wanna see DeNiro's ass as he gives it to that little shit punk.

c *winces.*

B

Naw, we gotta go low-key on the sex thing.

A *leans back, makes a «spoil-sport» face.*

c *leans forward.*

C

Hang on a minute. Where's the tension now that we've made the baby-killers straight?

A

The tension will be between DeNiro and that little shit-punk.

B

Yeah, they could be having problems at home. Like, the lawyer's boyfriend thinks the couple's guilty and DeNiro thinks the couple's innocent.

C

Hmm. What if it was the other the other way around? What if the lawyer thinks they're guilty and the lover thinks they're innocent? And then, at the last minute, the lawyer realizes they're innocent. But it's too late: they've just been found guilty.

A

And the last scene is DeNiro giving it to that puke little faggot.

B *ignores* A.

B

I got it! It's a chick lawyer.

A

Now we get Demi.

C

And what? Is she straight? Queer?

A

She's queer. And we get that old bag Eileen Brennan to play the lover.

C *winces.*

B

And Laurence Fishburne and Helena Bonham Carter to play the couple.

A

Who?

35

C
(*to* B)

Yeah. That'd get us our tension back.

A

Wait a minute. How does that get us our tension back?

C

It's an interracial couple.

A

Oh. So this Helen woman – she's black?

B

No. Laurence's black.

A

Oh.

C *turns towards* B.

C

But we ditch Eileen Brennan for Jennifer Jason Leigh.

B
(*thinks for a second*)

Yes! That's it. Perfect.

C *turns towards* A.

C

Perfect?

A *ponders.*

A
(*reluctantly*)

Yeah, okay. Perfect.
(*to* B, *angrily*)

Now write up the fuckin' treatment!

Camera pans right.

Two well-heeled white guys (early 30s). They've got the retro-lounge thing going. Although seated, you can tell that P *(to our left) is a much smaller man than* Q *(to our right). Also,* P *immediately seems «cooler» than* Q*. Both men are drinking cocktails. They must be slumming.*

P
(gesturing behind him)

Can you believe that?

Q

I don't know, but I'm impressed.

P *snickers.*

Q

No, really. They're totally right on. I've got something in development that's pretty fuckin' close.

P

What? A class-based, interracial, gay crime drama?

Q

No, no, no, no, no. A story about a bunch of working-class guys talking about making a movie.

P

For what reason?

Q

Whaddaya mean?

P

Well, why are they trying to make a movie?

Q
(shrugs)

To empower themselves, I guess.

37

P

Why don't they just go down to the video store and rent *Matewan* or something?

Q

Well, now that you mention it, that's sort of what got them started in the first place.

P

Naw, you're shittin' me. You're full of shit.

Q

No, really. But it wasn't *Matewan*. It was *Joe*.

P

Joe with Peter Boyle?

Q

Yeah.

P

So they're redneck types.

Q

I don't know. Is that what you got from *Joe*?

P

Oh yeah. Totally. They end up blowing away the hippies.

Q

Hmm. I saw it differently.

P

So what's the story?

Q
(glancing back at Table One)
I don't know. I'm still in revisions.

Camera pans right.

TABLE THREE

A legal book in the foreground. Torts or something. Two law clerks (late 20s). SHE's *black,* HE's *white. They're drinking red wine.* HE's *talking on a cellphone.* SHE *seems to be listening – but not to him.*

HE

Yeah, of course. Of course, Janey.... Yeah, for sure.... No, I don't see any problem with that.... No, of course we can have them ready for Monday.... No, thank *you*. I mean – if it wasn't for you, there's no way we would've.... No, I mean that, Janey. I really do. It was *you* who got us in at the DA in the first place. And it was *you* who brought us to Rupert's attention.... Yeah, but if it *wasn't* for you, then we'd never have gotten the chance to.... Okay.... (laughs) Yeah. Okay. Will do. Thanks Janey. Bye.

HE *snaps the phone shut, then gives up one of those jubilant «Yes!» gestures with his fist.* HE *turns to* SHE, *expecting an equally jubilant response.*

SHE *has her head turned slightly towards Table Two.*

HE *looks disappointed.*

HE

Weren't you listening?

SHE
(startled, turning towards HE)

Huh?

HE

We're in! Rupert wants to meet with us. He wants us to present our notes on the case against –

SHE

Sorry. I was distracted.

HE *looks over towards Table Two, then back at* SHE.

HE

What?

39

SHE

Nothing. Never mind. What did Janey —

HE
(*gesturing towards Table Two*)

What were they saying?

SHE

Nothing. They were just talking.

HE
(*indignant*)

About us? Were they talking about us?

SHE
(*firmly*)

No, okay? They're just a couple of stupid film guys.

HE

Look, if they're making disparaging remarks about us, I'm gonna —

HE *moves to get up.*

SHE *gestures for him to stay seated.*

SHE
(*indignant*)

Would you just cool it? And would you just stop it with this *us* stuff?

HE

Okay, okay. But just tell me if they said anything about the fact that you're black and I'm white and that we're sitting here having a drink. 'Cause if they did —

SHE

They weren't, okay?

HE

No, I mean it. I'm really sick and tired of —

SHE

Look, I said no, okay? Would you just listen for a minute? NO. N-O. No, they did not say anything about us. They were just talking about films, okay?
(*flustered*)
Jesus Christ! Why don't you ever —

HE
(*defensively*)

Okay, okay. Fine. That's all I wanted to know.

HE *crosses his arms and looks away, pouting.*

A beat.

SHE

But what if they were?

HE
(*turning back*)

Huh?

SHE

What if they *were* talking about us?

HE

Well, it would depend on what they said *exactly*. But —

SHE

Well, what if they said you were a stud because you were shagging a black chick?

HE
(*almost flattered*)

Did they really say that?

SHE

No.

HE
(*almost disappointed*)

Oh.

SHE

But what if they said I was a hooker and wondered what the fuck I was doing in here?

HE

Did they say that? Tell me the truth. Because if they did I'm gonna call them on it.

SHE

Like they would if they called you a stud for shagging some black chick?

HE

Well...*yeah*.

SHE

Whaddaya mean, *Well...yeah*? Like, it's okay if they call you a stud, but it's not okay if they call me a hooker?

HE

No, it's the same thing.

SHE

Obviously it *isn't* the same thing. You kinda got turned on when I said they called you a lucky guy, as if that somehow makes you a stud. But when I said they called me a whore, you got all indignant, as if that somehow makes you a loser, someone who either has to pay for sex or lives off the avails of —

HE

Wait a minute, now. You're the one leaping conclusions — not me.

SHE

No I'm not. You reacted differently.

HE

No I didn't.

SHE

You did! Be honest. It's okay. Just tell me the truth.

HE

Well...I don't know. I'm not sure.

Camera pans right.

TABLE FOUR

Two women. White. WOMAN 1 (LATE 40s) *and* WOMAN 2 (mid-20s). *Both are conservatively dressed, as if they've just come from work. They're drinking Caesars. And they're bored.*

WOMAN 1 *is lighting a cigarette.*

WOMAN 2

Anything good on TV tonight?

WOMAN 1

I don't know. I don't watch much TV anymore.

W2

Weren't you telling me last week you just bought a new Trinitron or something?

43

W1

Oh yeah. For videos though. I rented a whole bunch of videos yesterday, so I'll probably watch one of those.

W2

What videos did you get?

W1

Oh, you know, a bunch of stuff. There's this kid at the video store; he usually recommends about ten or so films and I just pick from that.

W2

So what did you get this time?

W1

Um, well, I got *Thelma & Louise*, which I hear is pretty good. And *Seven*, which is supposed to be scary. And something called *Mandingo*, a documentary about slavery, I think. And —

W2

Mandingo? That was just on cable. I watched a bit of that. It isn't a documentary though. More like a movie.

W1

Was it any good?

W2

I don't know. I fell asleep before it was over.

W1

So I guess it couldn't have been any good then?

W2

No, it was late. And it wasn't that bad. It's about an affair between a plantation owner's wife and his black slave. And the slave was played by that boxer from the seventies. I forget his name. Um —

W1

Ken Norton.

W2

Yeah.

W1

And did they, you know, show anything?

W2
(*excitedly*)

Well, it was on TV, so it was probably edited. But I remember there
was one scene, near the beginning, where the slaves were being
auctioned off, and this older sorta German woman, a widow, who
was bidding on this big, black guy, the Mandingo, reaches into
this guy's pants to, you know —

W1
(*giggling*)

Oh yeah.

W2

Yeah!

W1

And?

W2

Well, I guess she was satisfied 'cause she kept raising her bid.

They both laugh. Each take a sip from their drink.

W1
(*looking off*)

Gosh, I remember reaching into a black guy's pants once.

W2

Yeah?

W1

Oh yeah. This was years ago.

W2

And?

45

W1

Well, this was back when I was going to college ...

Cut to:

EXT. COLLEGE CAMPUS. 1967 – NIGHT

A young W1 and a young AFRICAN EXCHANGE STUDENT (20) walking hand-in-hand. W1 is wearing a pseudo-psychedelic «peasant» dress. The EXCHANGE STUDENT is wearing tan slacks and a short-sleeve shirt. They are talking to each other, smiling, but we only see their lips move.

W1
(*voice over*)

...and it was summertime. A really hot summer's night. And there was a big party for some exchange students and it kinda spilled out over campus. Oh yeah, I remember it well. I got to talking with this guy from Liberia. He was really interesting. Really good-looking: tall and slim, with a really nice face. And a really nice voice, too. Slow and deep. He was over here studying to be a doctor. And he was just...a really, really nice guy. So I kissed him.

The couple stop. They turn towards each other and kiss.

W2
(*voice over, to bartender*)

Yeah, I'll have another.
(*to W1*)

How 'bout you?
(*to BARTENDER*)

Make that two.

Cut to:

INT. A DIMLY LIT BAR – TABLE FOUR

W1

And we just got to fooling around, you know, out back of the
botany building, on the green. He was just really polite, not at all
aggressive. But he had this firmness about him, a real control,
you know. And I just put my hand down there and felt this huge
bulge. I mean, way bigger than any of the other guys I'd been
with. Not that there were many. And then I just thought, What the
hell? This is probably the only time in my life I'll ever get to do
something like this. So I undid his pants.

W2

And?

W1

And what?

W2

And then what happened?

W1

Well, you know, I reached my hand in and ...
(giggling)
...you know, it was hard. And I sorta played around with it.

W2

How big was it?

W1

Big.

W2

Like, a-foot-long big?

W1

Could've been. But I just remember it being really, really thick.

W2 *extends her arm towards* W1.

W2

Thicker than my wrist?

47

w1 reaches out and wraps her hand around w2's wrist. She closes her eyes, thinks for a second.

> W1

Thicker.

w2 picks up a couple of cocktail napkins and wraps them around her wrist. She extends her napkin-fortified wrist towards w1.

> W2

Thicker than this?

w1 wraps her hand around w2's napkin-fortified wrist.

A beat.

> W1

Yeah, more like that.

w2 wraps her own hand around her own wrist, shuts her eyes, then giggles.

> W2

Wow!
> *(opening her eyes)*

Was he uncircumcised?

Cut to:

EXT. COLLEGE CAMPUS — NIGHT

w1 and the EXCHANGE STUDENT break from their embrace. He takes a step back. They wave goodbye to each other, smiling. He backs out of the frame. She lingers, her smile slowly fading.

> W1
> *(voice over)*

Oh yeah. He was. I'd never been with a guy with a foreskin before.

                        W2
                    (*voice over*)
Did you go down on him?

                        W1
                    (*voice over*)
Oh god. I can't believe I'm talking about this.

                        W2
                    (*voice over*)
Why?

                        W1
                    (*voice over*)
I've never told anyone about this before.

                        W2
                    (*voice over*)
Why?

                        W1
                    (*voice over*)
I don't know. I mean – forget what you've heard about the sixties: things were pretty conservative back then. And once I got married I certainly didn't want my husband to know. And I certainly didn't tell any of our married friends.

                        W2
                    (*voice over*)
But did you go down on him?

Cut to:

INT. A DIMLY LIT BAR – TABLE FOUR

A beat.

W1 *begins a grin.*

W1

I did — yes.

W2

What was it like?

W1

Well, I couldn't get very much in.

w2's *eyes light up. She nods for more.*

W1

I mean, the head was like…

w1 *looks around the table, then down at her hand, clenching it, raising it slightly.*

…like the size of my fist.

w2 *reaches out, closing her hand over* w1 *'s fist. She's impressed.*

W2

Ho-ly shit!

W1

Yeah. My jaw sure hurt after that one.

w1 *rubs her jaw.*

In fact…

(*laughing*)

…I think that might be the reason why it clicks.

w1 *opens and shuts her mouth a couple of times.*

Can you hear that?

w1 *opens and shuts her mouth once more.*

My jaw clicking?

W2

What about his balls? Big?

W1

Huge. The biggest bag I've ever seen. And when we were having
intercourse, when he put it in from behind me, they would swing
right up and slap against my clit. That was the first orgasm I ever
had from intercourse. His balls swinging up on my clit like that.

W2

So you *had* intercourse?!

W1

Oh yeah. It took a long time, though. I really had to trust him – on
account of his size. Plus the fact that we weren't using a condom.
But he knew what he was doing. He was *reeeeal* pro.

W2

Did he go down you?

W1

Oh yeah. For about a half-hour.

W2

Wow.

W1

That was one of the best half-hours of my life.
(*laughs*)
It was great. And he didn't rush it, either. He was really gentle.
And it wasn't just all tongue. He was really good with his fingers,
too. He had really soft hands.
(*looking away*)
Oh yeah. Every now and then, when it's summer, and if
somebody's cutting the grass, I can smell him. Just the two of us.

W2

Did you have an orgasm from him going down on you?

W1

Oh yeah. A bunch of 'em. Little ones. One after another. But what I remember best was what I saw in my head. Lying there on my back, looking up at the stars. It was like I was floating in space. And then, all of a sudden, the stars began to grow together until finally it was just this intense, surging white light. And then I looked down at my body, because, for some reason, it felt like it was, you know, melting away. And sure enough, it was. It was gone. It was all light. White light. But I didn't feel scared, 'cause I really trusted this guy. And I remember reminding myself of that at that moment. And then just as I did that all these colours started swirling – yellows, oranges, light blues. And each colour had its own tone, right? Its own flavour. Yeah, I had this great feeling for all these little colours.

W2

And then what happened?

W1

Then I kinda snapped out of it, 'cause he stopped going down on me.

W2

Is that when you started having intercourse?

W1

Well, he was getting kinda soft, so I started trying to get him hard again with my hand. But I wasn't getting anywhere with it. And I didn't really want to put my mouth around it again 'cause it was just way too fat. So I was getting kinda frustrated 'cause I really wanted to, you know, get it on with this guy.

W2

So then what did you do?

W1

Well, he just kinda took over — which was great because it was really sexy watching him get himself hard — which turned me on even more. I mean, there I was, lying on my back, the little peasant dress I had to beg my mother to buy me hiked up under my shoulders, legs spread-eagle, and this magnificent man, with his back to the light, rubbing the curve back into this great, big, beautiful cock he was about to put inside me.

W2

His cock was curved?!

W1

Yeah.

W2

Gosh, I've never seen one of those before.

W1

Yeah, I didn't really notice at first. But when he knelt down in front of me, when he started to get hard again, it seemed to have this curve in it. Like a banana.

W2

Did it hurt when he put it in you?

W1

Oh yeah. But just a little. I mean — he knew what he was doing, right? He sorta rubbed it against me for awhile, which —

W2

So he put it in slow?

W1

Of course. He had to. I mean, he knew he had a huge cock. And he was studying medicine, so he knew he couldn't just ram it in there. In fact, once he started to put it inside me, he sorta let me take over. He told me right off to coach him.

W2

Did he actually say that? Did he actually use the word *coach*?

W1

What he said was, um, well, it was something like:
                                 (*imitatively, in a low voice*)
Now, baby, you just relax and tell me what you want and I'll follow orders. He actually said that: *follow orders*. Then he said: I don't wanna hurt you now. I just wanna make you feel reeeeal goooood. I want the both of us to feeeeeel reeeeal goooood.

W2

Oh-my-god.

W1

And then he just kinda eased it in.

W2

All of it at once?!

W1

No, no. He just sorta pushed the tip of it in and out – which, I admit, did hurt a little. But then I was aching for it! After that I relaxed a bit, and then he just kinda pushed the whole head of it inside me, which was more a mental shock than a physical one. After that it felt great.

W2

Whaddaya mean, a *mental shock*?

W1

Well, it was like – you remember being a kid and eating a food that you'd never eaten before and sometimes, say, if the food comes in a shape you're not used to, and you're not sure whether you should cut it in half or just put the whole thing in your mouth, and how sometimes you just swallow and it kinda surprises your throat?

W2

Sort of.

W1

Well, say if the food is something like a meatball and you put the whole thing in your mouth and start chewing and you realize that it's too big for your mouth but you're determined to swallow it anyway rather than spit it out? And then once you start swallowing, you realize how big it really is? And that it's kinda startling? But that it doesn't physically hurt?

W2

Yeah, yeah. Now I know what you mean. I remember seeing my cousin do that once at the dinner table.

Cut to:

INT. W2'S COUSIN'S KITCHEN. 1977 — NIGHT

A young girl at the dinner table, her eyes bulging out. She seems to be choking on her food. A man (her father?) is behind her, slapping her back.

W1
(*voice over*)

Well, that's kinda what it was like with this guy's cock. The head of it just kinda popped through. And then he just kinda pushed it back-and-forth, side-to-side, real gentle, till I finally caught up with it.

Cut to:

INT. DIMLY LIT BAR — TABLE FOUR

W2

Then what?

W1

Then he asked me if I wanted a little bit more, and I said yeah, sure. So he pushed it in a little further, then stopped, letting it slide back a little. Boy, I remember really wanting the whole thing bad at that point. I asked him to push it back it in, and he did, and I remember digging my heels in the ground and pushing my hips hard toward him. Then he pulled back hard, almost pulling it right out, and gave me a «*Whoa, baby, I don't wanna come too quick,*» so I just sorta lay back a bit, to get a sense of his pace.

W2

It doesn't sound like you were really coaching him, does it?

W1

Well, no. Not at the beginning. But once he got used to my pussy I had to start telling him what I wanted – and what I didn't want. I mean, at one point he was really starting to go at it and I had to push him back.

W2

Did he have the whole thing in at that point?

W1

God no! Barely half. But that's where his cock was at its fattest, see? He could have ripped me apart if he went any further.

W2

And you weren't scared?

W1

Not really, no. He was *that* considerate. I mean, he was really afraid he was gonna come too fast. And that's pretty considerate, if you ask me.

W2

Yeah.

W1

He knew what he was doing. He was really good. And his shape — yeah, he felt really good inside me.

W2

Wow. So you took the whole thing?

W1

Oh yeah — eventually. But just as I was getting into it, he pulled out and turned me around.

W2

Yeah?

W1

And I was, like, really woozy. My body felt really, really heavy without his cock inside me. Like I was drunk or something. But he was great. He just reached underneath and lifted me onto my hands and knees. I remember looking back between my legs as he pulled down his pants a little more — and the light from the botany building on his balls like that. Oh god, it was such a turn-on.

W2

Then he put it in from behind?

W1

Then he put it in from behind. He put about half of it in real fast, in one go – any more and I woulda passed out – and then he pulled back real slow. That felt good. And I told him so. Then he pushed it back in, a little more each time, then pulled out real slow again. And he kept on doing that till he had it all the way in. Then he just kinda stopped.

W2

With the whole thing in?

W1

Yeah. And he kinda kept it there. And it was throbbing away like a heart – or he was flexing it or something. I don't know. But it was in there big time. Nice 'n' tight. There wasn't much room for anything else.

W2

Didn't it hurt, then? I mean, that's a deep-penetration position.

W1

Yeah. And believe me: it was all I could do to hang on.

W2

Well, you said your orgasm came from his balls slapping against you?

W1

Oh yeah. Well, after awhile he pulled it back a bit and started moving it in and out. Real slow at first. Then he started giving it. And did that ever feel good! Then I realized what felt so good was his balls knocking against my clitoris like that. And as soon as I realized that I started to orgasm.

W2

Did he come, too?

W1

Not right away.

W2

Did he come inside you?

W1

Are you kidding?! We didn't have a condom! No, he just pulled it out real fast, which totally caught me off guard. And then I sorta rolled over and watched him jerk off. When he was about to come he turned to his side and shot.

W2

Was there lots?

W1

Of ejaculate? Oh yeah. Buckets! It was flying all over the place. I could see it all against the light of the botany building. I remember thinking each ejaculation looked like a...a bunch of grasshoppers or something. It was really beautiful.

W2

Wow. And did he make a noise when he came?

W1

Just this low *ohhh* sound.

W2

Oh wow. And then what?

W1

We just lay there and talked. Then he walked me back to the party.

W2

What did you talk about?

W1
(*shrugs*)

Stuff...*school*. Maybe some personal stuff.

W2

Like what?

W1
(*laughing*)

Hey, stop being so nosy, would ya?!

w2 *smiles.*

W2

Ah, c'mon. You can tell me.

W1

Nope. No way. That stuff's none of your business.

W2

Did you ever see him again?

W1
(*sadly*)

No.

W2

Why not?

W1

He went back to Liberia the next day.

W2

Well, would you have seen him again if he didn't go back?

W1

I don't know.

W2

What if this happened today? In the '90s? Would you have seen him again if he wasn't going back?

W1

Not necessarily. But he did send a letter, though. About a couple of weeks after he left. A really nice one, too. He didn't mention anything about our night together. He just told me about how happy he was to be back home and stuff, and all the things he wanted to do there, and that he hoped I was happy, too. And that was good enough for me.

Camera pans left.

TABLE THREE

HE

Yeah.

SHE

Yeah what?

HE

Yeah, you're right. I did react differently.

SHE

Well, *yeah*, I know that. But do you know why, though? Do you know why you reacted differently?

HE

Well, I suppose it was 'cause I was flattered by the idea that I was, you know, pretty lucky to be, you know, fucking you or, uh, I don't know, having some kind of, what, *sway* over you or something.

SHE
(*sarcastically*)

Because all black women are, you know, horny and promiscuous and, ah, I don't know, submissive and like being under —

HE

Okay, okay —

SHE
(*angrily*)

No! Don't «okay, okay» me! I have to put up with this kinda shit every day. And here I am getting a chance to talk about it and you're dismissing me because you think just because you feel bad about it that somehow that's enough. What about how I feel about it? Don't you wanna know how all this makes me feel?

HE

Yeah, well, I already know you feel pretty shitty about it.

SHE

Do you wanna know what it's like to be a young black woman
walking down the street at night? In a city where everyone thinks
you're a prostitute? Or a drug addict? Or a gangster? Do you wanna
know what it's like trying to hail a cab at two o'clock in the
morning? After you've been waiting around for twenty minutes?
When you know that cab is gonna go right past you and pick up the
white woman coming out of the building half a block away?

HE

I can imagine it makes you feel pretty shitty.

SHE

Of course it makes me feel shitty! But it's more than that. It's not
like it goes away when I get home, when I have to hear about it
from my brother's point-of-view. Or like when I was younger,
when I used to see it in my parent's faces – my parents who never
talked about it, who just accepted it as a fact of life.

HE

Yeah, I guess it sorta affects you when it's not actually happening.

SHE

Yeah, but it's *always actually happening*! You take that hurt and
pile it up on top of all the other hurts and the weight is so fucking
unbearable that after awhile it's all you can do to avoid those
situations where that kinda shit happens. And then it gets to the
point where you get like your parents, where you just stay inside
all day, where you only go out and do the things that other black
people do, where you do jobs where you don't have to deal with
white people, the kinda jobs that white people don't want to do.

HE *nods slowly, head bowed.*

She sighs, letting go of her shoulders.

SHE

Thank you.

62

HE
(*looking up*)

For what?

SHE

For not saying anything.

HE

Well, I was just listening.

SHE

Were you? Were you really?

HE

Yeah.

SHE

Well, that's all I really wanted you to do. Just listen. And maybe think about what I've had to say — how I feel.

HE

Yeah, well, I guess what you've said sorta reminds me of some of the feelings I had growing up working-class, going to a middle-class school —

SHE

That's not the same thing.

HE

Well, I kinda think it is. It's all about oppression, isn't it? Difference?

SHE

Yeah, it's oppression. And, yes, it's difference. But it's different. And it's different because you're not a woman and you're not black.

HE
(*defensively*)

So what you're saying is that because you grew up black and a woman and poor that you somehow had it harder than me? And that because of that hardship you are somehow *better* than me? Me, who's *merely* working-class. Me, who's *merely* one-eighth Indian?

SHE *looks confused for a second, then begins to laugh.*

HE *knows his logic is bad, and throws his hands up.*

SHE *laughs harder at his «I give up» gesture.*

SHE

One-eighth Indian...?

HE
(*playing along*)

Yeah!

SHE

Which eighth?

HE

My great-grandfather's second wife. She was a Seneca.

SHE *laughs again, shaking her head, then leans towards him, smiling.*

SHE
(*sincerely*)

Look. Lemme tell you something. I grew up black, I grew up a woman, and I grew up working-class. And you wanna know something? I am still black. I am still a woman. And I am still working-class. And I'm proud of that. And, no, I am not saying that I'm better than you. I'm just —

HE
(*seriously*)

I think you are, though. I think that's what you're *really* saying.

SHE

No I'm not. And what's this *better* shit all about, anyway? How am *I* in a *better* position than *you*?

HE

Well, maybe *better* isn't the word. Maybe I mean —

SHE
(*facetiously*)

Self-righteous?

HE

I dunno. Yeah.

SHE

How do you equate *self-righteous* with *better*?

HE

Well, it's like you have the moral high-ground here. And I find that really hard to argue with.

SHE
(*impatiently*)

Because I'm a black woman?

> HE

Well…

> SHE

Or because of your white male guilt?

> HE

Because of the white male guilt I've been conditioned into.

> SHE

Conditioned by.

> HE

Yeah.

> SHE

And that conditioning process is coming from?

> HE
> (*shrugs*)

I don't know. All over, I guess.

Camera pans left.

TABLE TWO

B *from Table One is sitting with* P *at Table Two.*

> P
> (*in mid-sentence*)

…so what you gotta remember is that a treatment is really just an outline — no more than twenty pages. It's a little more elaborate than a synopsis; it should contain scenes, some dialogue, and some character sketches.

> B

Well, we're doin' something feature-length, something Hollywood, so I guess we're eventually looking at, what, ninety pages for a finished script?

P

Yeah. About that. But you also gotta remember that the key to
your story – especially if it's for Hollywood – is pacing. The first
section is the set-up; that's about a quarter of your story. The next
section is the confrontation; and that's about half your story right
there. And the last bit is the resolution, which is roughly the same
length as the set-up.

B

And a page of script is pretty much the same as a minute of film,
right?

P

Approximately, yeah.

B

Okay. We've pretty much got the set-up figured out. And we know
the confrontation part is going to be centred around the court
room stuff. So I guess what we need to know is how to end it.

P *nods.*

B *shrugs.*

P

Well, how do you *want it* to end?

B

Well, we're not totally sure yet. I mean, it's gonna depend on the
casting.

P
(amused)

No, no, no, no, no. You gotta write the screenplay first.

B

Yeah, well, that's really hard to do without knowing who these
people are gonna be.

P *shakes his head, confused.*

                              B

Well, that's what we've done in the past. I make the pitch, then my
boss starts to fill in the actors. Then the story changes, and the
other guy I work with sorta fixes it, then I write up the treatment,
then my boss approves it, then I write the screenplay. And that's
what I thought we had today, except my boss came back from the
can and started fiddling with the casting again. He really wants
DeNiro and that Leonardo DiCaprio guy.

                              P
                          (stunned)

Okay.

                              B
                          (nodding)

Yep.

                              P

And how many screenplays *have* you guys written?

                              B

Uhhh — since I've been on this crew — about twenty. But before I
came along my boss and the other guy we work with — they prob'ly
wrote about two hundred.

                              P
                         (surprised)

Two hundred feature-length screenplays?!

                              B

Yeah, give-or-take.

                              P

And they're all different from each other?

                              B

Oh yeah. Some are action films, some are love stories, and some
are adapted from books. The last ten or so have been courtroom
dramas.

P

Right.

B

Yeah, when I first started my boss took me over to his place and
showed me a whole stack. A whole mountain of screenplays!
Yeah. The first ones he did on his own – all of 'em pornos. And he
had these really funny storyboards to go along with them – you
know, stick-men...

    (gesturing, a finger in and out of a curled hand)

...doing it.

P

And these were all finished screenplays?

B

Yeah. The first one he did was about four hundred pages long. It
was all about this riot at a youth detention centre. Some island
somewhere. And it was called, um, *A Nice Mentor*, which he told
me was a, uh – What are those things called where the letters
from one thing make up the letters to, uh –

P

An anagram.

B

Right! An anagram. *A Nice Mentor* is an anagram for «Ancient
Rome.»

P

Did you read it?

B

Sure. It was pretty funny. All about these guys fucking each other
up the ass and stuff.

P

And your boss – was he the Nice Mentor?

B

Sort of. He told me once how he used to work at one of those detention centres when he was younger. But nah, he's not a queer or anything.

P

Right.

B

Anyway, he's got a dirty sense of humour. But that's just the way he is, right? And, I mean, me and the other guy we work with, we just accept that as part of his personality.

P

That other guy you work with —

B

Yeah.

P

How long has he been working with your boss?

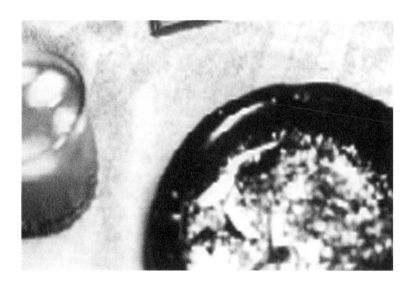

B
(*thinks*)

About twelve years.

P

And he's sorta the fix-it guy?

B

Yeah, the script-doctor. He usually makes sense of everything.
He's got a Masters in English, you know.

P

Really.

B

Oh yeah. But try getting a job with a Masters in English! He says
he knows people with PhDs that are still waiting tables.

P

Sure, I believe it. Say, you said you've adapted books. Which
ones?

B

Catcher in the Rye, On the Road, The Electric Kool-Aid Acid Test -- oh,
and some letters to these fag magazines my boss said he found on
our route once.

P

You don't believe he found them.

B

Well, he hardly ever leaves the truck, so I don't know how he
found them.

P

Do you think he bought them?

B

Nah, he's not really like that. He probably got them at the dump. He probably told us he found them on the route 'cause he's always trying to make us feel like we've missed something good. We're always finding stuff on our route.

Camera pans left.

Q *from Table Two is seated with* A *and* C *at Table One.* Q *is under attack from* A. C *grins as he listens.*

A *is pointing his finger violently at* Q.

A
(*in mid-sentence*)

...and that's why they're making shitty movies, and that's why the studios are losing money, and that's why Hollywood is so fucked up!

Q *is bemused, though a bit overwhelmed.*

Q

Hey, you'll get no argument from me. I agree with everything you're saying. But as I've already told you, my partner and I don't work with the majors.

A

Yeah, not at the moment. But what happens when those Disney fucks come along and want to buy one of your scripts? What happens then? What happens when they start waving the jake around? Are you gonna go, *Ah, shucks, I'll take your money but ya gotta promise not to screw with my story?* No, you're gonna take the money and run. And you're not gonna care if they turn your civil rights drama into *Beach Blanket Bingo.*

Q *is shaking his head, giggling. He can't believe this guy's for real.*

Q

I don't think that's gonna happen.

A

But how do you know, though?! How do you know that some
screenplay you've just sold to some indie art fag isn't gonna get
flipped to some snot-nosed actor who wants to direct his first
buddy flick?

Q
(*smiling*)

Nope. It ain't gonna happen. It ain't gonna happen because the
films my partner and I make aren't mainstream films. They just
don't have the same narrative structures as mainstream films.
Besides, we *make* the films we write.

c *leans forward, elbows on the table. He is grinning.*

C

So you guys are more the Stan Brakhage-type.

A *makes a sour face. It's not so much a I-don't-like-Stan Brakhage face as
an I-don't-know-Stan Brakhage face.*

Q
(*pleasantly surprised*)

Hey, there you go. Stan Brakhage. Now there's a sexy filmmaker.

C

I met him once, a few years ago, at a screening in Toronto.

A *shakes his head in disgust, pushing back from the table.*

Q

Cool.

C

Yeah. It *was* cool. Does Brakhage inform your work?

Q
Well...*yeah*. He has a certain, um, lyric quality that we admire. Him and people like – you know – Carolee Schneemann, Derek Jarman...

c *nods knowingly.*

...I mean, we don't scratch up the print or anything. But on a couple of films we've, you know, taken felt pens to the emulsion and stuff. But more than that, we just like the way his films flow. It suits the subject matter we tend to work with pretty good.

C
And what's that?

Q
The subject matter? Pornography. We make pornographic films.

A *comes to life like a startled dog.*

A
Pornos! You guys make pornos!

Q
Yeah.

C
You mean erotic films.

Q
Nope. We make no bones about it. It's hardcore porno.

A *is so excited he can hardly speak. Like a dog drooling over a steak.*

A
I, ah, I've got some, ah –

C
(*speaking over* A)
So where do your films get shown?

                                    Q
Privately. Mostly Europe. We sell direct to collectors. We shoot,
print, and cut in 35. Most of our work is commissioned.

                                    C
How does *that* work?

                                    Q
In all kinds of ways. There's this one guy we know in Paris, a
German guy – the Baron, we call him – and he usually finds these
people on his travels and sends them to us – along with a bunch
of money. He has all these notes about what he wants us to do with
them and we just sort of write it into something.

A *finally composes himself. He has a serious look on his face – the kind of
look one adopts when they want to be taken seriously.*

                                    A
                         (*clearing his throat*)
I am very interested in meeting this Baron guy.

                                    Q
Sorry. We're sworn to secrecy.

                                    A
Well, it's just that, uh, I've got some screenplays of my own lying
around and, uh, you know, there might be something of interest
there.

Q *nods along, then, realizing he has to say something, quickly shrugs his
shoulders, throwing his hands up.*

                                    Q
Sorry, can't help you there. Wish I could, but I can't.

A *makes a dejected face, then slumps back, turning away. His facial
expression suggests he's plotting a new approach.*

                                    C
How did you guys get started making porno?

A *assumes an inquiring face, as if it was he who asked the question.*

Q

Well, we started out making experimental shorts at film school, at UCLA. We got a bit of attention, won some awards, then went to Europe. One of our earlier films, a little thing called *Such*, was a bit of a take-off on that scene in Antonioni's *Zabriskie Point* – the one with all those naked couples writhing in the desert – except way more explicit. Anyway, *Such* opened a lot of doors for us – particularly in Eastern Europe. There's a lot of pornography coming out of Hungary – and there's a group over there that uses pornography as social criticism. And they saw some of our work and invited us over. And that's where we met the Baron, at a porno trade show in Budapest. We've been working for him exclusively ever since.

A

So it's like you had to have something made in order for somebody to become interested?

Q *is trying to take* A *seriously, taking delight in the fact that he's about to restate the obvious.*

Q

Yeah, we had to make a film in order for somebody to be interested in us as filmmakers.

C

Do you still produce work for public screening?

Q

No, not really. I'm perfectly happy being on the Baron's payroll, making pictures for the Baron.
(*slowly, deviously*)
My partner, however...
(*looking over his shoulder*)
...is always itchin' to do more public stuff.

A *looks towards Table Two. He gets up and exits the frame (towards Table Two).*

Once A *is out of the picture,* C *leans a little closer towards* Q.

C
(smiling)

You're Faron Whitter, aren't you?

Q *smiles like he might be.*

C

And your partner — your partner's Barry Tate, right?

Q*'s smile broadens.*

Camera pans left.

TABLE FOUR

An intensely big black man, a LIBERIAN, *is standing beside a seated* W2. *He is the same man we saw earlier with* W1, *except this time he is attired in traditional Malinke (Mandingo) clothing.*

W2 *looks at* W1, *makes an inquiring face.*

W1 *shrugs a «whatever.»*

W2 *looks up into the face of the* LIBERIAN, *then reaches into a slit at the hip of his djellabah.*

W2, *still looking up into the face of the* LIBERIAN, *begins to fondle the man's genitals.*

W2*'s breath is heavy.*

W1 *lights a cigarette.*

The LIBERIAN *stands, oblivious.*

He looks into the camera.

Then...

LIBERIAN
(*slowly, deeply*)

My name is Sao Bosa. I am the great-great-great-great-*great*-grandson of the first Sao Bosa. And the ninth Sao Bosa! Yes, I am the ninth – that is, Doctor Sao Bosa, the Ninth, to you, my friend.

The first Sao Bosa. He was leader of the Condo confederation in Bopulu. A great, great man. A Mandingo! Oh, though he was raised by a Gbandi chief, he was Mandingo through and through.

Yes, the first Sao Bosa. Between 1800 and 1830 he had influence over thirty towns in central Liberia, from the northern edges of the savanna right down to the Atlantic Ocean. All the Loma, Fula, Gola, Vai – even the Mandingo! – they were all under the influence of the first Sao Bosa.

EXTREME CLOSE-UP ON LIBERIAN'S FACE
(*whispering to the camera*)

And you know something else? My great-great-great-great-*great*-grandfather? He had a cock two feet long. Oh yes! And what's more! He had many wives. And he had many children, too.

Cut to:

EXT. COLLEGE CAMPUS. 1967 – NIGHT

w1 is standing where we left her. Her smile is gone. She looks longingly at something off camera. We hear the fading click of footsteps.

LIBERIAN
(*voice over*)

Sao Bosa, the first – he was a slave trader. Oh, he was wheeling-and-dealing slaves long before the British came along, long before they abolished slavery in 1806 – when they took their slaving underground, where the big money lay. Oh yes!

EXT. A WEALTHY RESIDENTIAL STREET — NIGHT

The traditionally dressed LIBERIAN *walks down the empty sidewalk, his back to the camera.*

> LIBERIAN
> (*voice over*)
>
> And when those boats from America came! In 1820. Sao Bosa — he was there. The American Colonial Society. They came on their boats to land on Dazoe, to sip fresh water from the Mesurado. Oh yes! Sao Bosa was there to see this: the American black woman in her apron dress; the American black man in his stockings and tails. And all that talk of repatriation. All that talk of a black middle-class.

The LIBERIAN *laughs.*

INT. A DIMLY LIT BAR — TABLE FOUR

> LIBERIAN
>
> Sao Bosa — he did not side with the Dei. He did not attack the settlers. Oh no! He knew what those settlers wanted. And he was just the man to give it to them. He would give them access to trade routes, because he knew that they would never be content to just grow vegetables. And it would be easy — as easy as not doing something can sometimes be. Oh yes! He said, Away with you, Todo. Away with you, Konko. Go away, King Long Peter. Which they did.
>
> This Sao Bosa — he was so smart. He could see it all coming. He would do well for his people. He would give them all head starts.

Camera pans left.

TABLE THREE

HE *is sitting alone, playing with a piece of paper or something. Upon closer inspection we see he is folding a circular cardboard coaster into a square dish shape.* HE *kisses from his mouth a chewed-up piece of gum, taking it between thumb and forefinger and dropping it into his sculpture.* HE *then folds the sculpture in half, pressing down hard until he feels the gum take hold. The new shape is rectangular.* HE *examines his work, then absently tosses it in the ashtray.*

SHE *enters the frame and sits down.*

> SHE
>
> I just talked to my brother. He's comin' down to join us for a drink.

> HE
> *(faking enthusiasm)*
>
> Great.

A beat.

> Your older brother, right?

> SHE
>
> I only have the one.

> HE
>
> Oh. Right. Well…how's he doing these days?

> SHE
>
> You can ask him yourself; he'll be here in a few minutes.

SHE *takes a sip from her drink.*

> But yeah, he's fine. Yeah, he just got a promotion. And he's been seeing this guy for awhile now, and it's starting to look serious. So yeah, he's doin' great.

HE *has been nodding along, eager to prove his interest.*

> HE
> *(making conversation)*
>
> So he's seein' a guy?

SHE
(*suspiciously*)

Yeah. I've told you my brother's gay.

HE
(*as if startled*)

Oh yeah. Yeah, you did tell me. He was seeing a guy from France, right?

SHE

Belgium.

HE

Belgium.

SHE

Henri.

HE

Right. Henri, the ballet dancer.

SHE

Right. But his new boyfriend's name is Ramòn.

HE

Sure. Ramòn. Got it.

A beat.

SHE

And Ramòn's gonna join us as well.

HE

No problem.

A beat.

SHE *takes another sip, then, matter-of-factly:*

SHE

Ramòn's a boxer.

HE *laughs. It is the worst kind of laugh. The kind of laugh where the person doing the laughing is trying to keep the laugh inside — where the laugh happens just as the laugher is taking a sip off a drink. It begins with a spew and ends with a cough.*

SHE
(disgusted)

Fuck you.

HE *tries to compose himself.*

HE

I'm sorry. I really am. It's just the way you said it. The way you looked at me when you said that he's a...
(laughing, coughing)
...a boxer.
(gasping)
I mean — it's the way you said it, not what you said.

SHE

Whaddaya mean, the way I said it?!

HE

It's just something you do from time to time, and it really cracks me up. That deadpan way you have of saying things.

SHE *says nothing. She just stares at him, unconsciously making the deadpan face he seems to find so funny.*

HE *points at her and begins to laugh again.*

HE

You're doing it right now!

SHE *ignores him. Then something catches her eye. She looks beyond him, then smiles, waving.*

HER BROTHER *and* RAMÒN *enter the frame and stop.*

HER BROTHER *(late 30s), is dressed in expensive casual clothes.*

RAMÒN *is a tall, good-looking Hispanic man (early 20s).*

HER BROTHER

Hey, baby sister.

SHE *stands up and hugs* HER BROTHER.

RAMÒN *and* HE *acknowledge each other with nods.*

SHE

Hey, big brother.

SHE *and* HER BROTHER *hug, making mm-mmm noises.*

HE *quickly looks back at* RAMÒN, *as if he recognizes him.*

HER BROTHER
(*to* SHE)

You look good!

RAMÒN, *aware that he is being looked at, slowly turns to look at* HE.
RAMÒN *smiles politely.*

HE *returns the smile, then looks away.* HE *is thinking.*

SHE
(*to* HER BROTHER)

Like you knew I would!

HER BROTHER *gestures with his thumb behind him, to* RAMÒN.

HER BROTHER
(*to* SHE)

You two know each other, right?

Both SHE *and* RAMÒN *exchange yeses and hellos.*

Both SHE *and* HER BROTHER *turn to* HE.

HE *has exchanged his thinking face for an open one.* HE *gets up and says hi to* HER BROTHER.

HER BROTHER *grunts.*

HE *remains open, unfazed.*

HE
(*to* SHE)

Uh, excuse me. I've gotta make a quick call.

HE *takes another quick look at* RAMÒN.

SHE *throws* HE *a confused face.*

HE *moves between* SHE *and* HER BROTHER.

HER BROTHER *scowls after him.*

SHE *shakes off her confused face for a smiling one.*

SHE *turns back to face* HER BROTHER.

HER BROTHER *gestures after* HE, *as if to say, «What's he doing here?»*

SHE *makes an «Oh well» face.*

RAMÒN *reaches out of frame to grab a chair.*

The three of them sit down at the same time.

SHE *remains camera-left,* HER BROTHER *camera-right.* RAMÒN *is in the middle.*

> SHE
>
> So what's new?

> HER BROTHER
> (*to* SHE, *happily*)
>
> Well, we've got some news.

> SHE
> (*joking*)
>
> You're gonna have a baby.

RAMÒN *laughs.*

> HER BROTHER
> (*annoyed*)
>
> No, no, no, no, *no.*

> SHE
> (*concerned*)
>
> What then? Is it bad?

HER BROTHER *winks at* RAMÒN, *then to* SHE...

> HER BROTHER
> (*smiling*)
>
> We've just bought a condo.

SHE *opens her face. A happy squeak pops out.*

> SHE
>
> Great! Where?

> HER BROTHER
>
> Near the market.

SHE *beams at* RAMÒN, *then back at* HER BROTHER.

> SHE
>
> Congratulations, you guys! So when do you take possession?

HER BROTHER
(*proudly*)

Next month.

SHE

Wow. Have you, uh – have you told Mom yet?

HER BROTHER *looks down, almost ashamed.*

HER BROTHER
(*quietly*)

No.

SHE
(*sympathetically*)

Aw.

RAMÒN
(*in broken English*)

Your mother, she does not know your brother is gay.

SHE
(*smiling weakly*)

Yes, Ramòn, I know that.

A beat.

HER BROTHER *reaches up and pinches the bridge of his nose, shutting his eyes. He is pained.*

SHE *reaches over, takes* HER BROTHER*'s other hand in hers.*

> SHE
>
> You gotta tell her *some* day.

> RAMÒN
>
> We know.

HER BROTHER *snaps out of it, straightening up, looking around, angrily…*

> HER BROTHER
> (*to* SHE)
>
> So what's What's-His-Face doing here?

SHE *sighs hard, her shoulders drop.*

> SHE
>
> Aw, don't start. Not now.

> HER BROTHER
>
> What do you see in that guy, anyway? Why are you always hangin' with *him*?

> SHE
>
> We're study partners. And we happen to be at the DA together, okay?

> HER BROTHER
>
> Ah, that goof is *sooo* Velveeta! You're dissin' yourself girl just bein' seen in his company.

> SHE
>
> Look, I don't wanna get into this again. He's a good study partner. He helped me out big-time when we were at law school. And now we've got bar exams coming up and —

> HER BROTHER
> (*mocking her in a bitched-up tone*)

And you had a fling with him once, but it's over.

SHE *throws her hands up, leaning back in her chair.*
> (*calmly*)

Look, sister, I know, I know. But dontcha think it's time you moved on? You gotta get up and go from this —

SHE *leans forward, stabbing her index finger at a point on the table.*

> SHE
> (*angrily*)

Look, who the fuck gives you the right to —

HER BROTHER *leans in, ready to engage her.*

> RAMÒN
> (*pushing them apart*)

Ah, excuse me. Excuse me! But I did not take the evening off to listen to you two argue, okay then?

SHE *and* HER BROTHER *stop. They both lean back, hard.* SHE *crosses her arms. Both look at each other with cross expressions.*

> HER BROTHER
> (*lightening up*)

Alright, alright.

> SHE
> (*still a bit pissed*)

Thanks, Ramòn.

> RAMÒN
> (*to* SHE, *slowly, with difficulty*)

Your brother tells me you will be finished your training soon, and that you will become a professional lawyer.

> SHE

Yes, Ramòn. In three months. I write my bar exams in three months.

RAMÒN *makes an interested, please-continue face.*

> Then, I guess, I'll have to find a job. I mean, I don't think I want to spend the rest of my life at the District Attorney's office. But then again, law jobs are pretty hard to find right now. Every third person's a lawyer these days.

SHE *and* HER BROTHER *give* RAMÒN *their full attention, like they would to a stutterer.*

RAMÒN

Yes. I have heard that. So maybe then...you will become...a waiter?

Both SHE *and* HER BROTHER *look at each other, confused, before clueing in to* RAMÒN's *corny joke. They turn to* RAMÒN *and laugh.*

RAMÒN *laughs.*

They are all laughing.

HE *enters the frame, camera-left, smiling.*

HE
(happily confused)

What's so funny?

SHE
(coming down from her laughter)

Oh, just my new career.

HE *is still happily confused.*

SHE
(looking at RAMÒN)

As a waiter.

HE *shakes off his confusion, trying to go with the flow.*

HE

Well, if you're gonna be a waiter, then I suggest you learn from the best. I've just made reservations for four at Tulane's. On me.

RAMÒN

Ah, Tulane's! Very nice.

HE
(*to* SHE)

Seven-thirty okay?

SHE *makes an excited face, then quickly glances over at* HER BROTHER.

HER BROTHER *scowls.*

Camera pans left.

TABLE TWO

P *and* Q *are seated in their original positions. They are very excited speaking quickly in hushed tones.*

Q
(*in mid-sentence*)

...and then when I told them we made pornos, I swear the old guy almost knocks the table over with a boner.

P

That kid has got his shit together, man. I mean, he's a little out there, but –

Q

But it's the *other* guy that *really* knows his shit. He knows tons about film. And not just Hollywood. Schneemann, Brakhage, Jarman. D'ya know he's got his Masters in –

P

I don't doubt it. He's the fuckin' script doctor, for fuck's sake.

They both giggle.

Q

But get this: he thinks we're Whitter and Tate.

P *makes a «no-fuckin'-kidding» kind of face.*

P

Who's who?

Q

I'm Whitter, you're Tate.

P
(*jokingly*)

But I wanna be Whitter.

Q *stifles a laugh.*

Q

Tough shit.

P *stifles a laugh.*

Q

We gotta get this down, man. This is gonna make a great film. I already dropped a couple of clues to the old guy that you were looking do some…
(*making quotation gestures*)
…serious stuff –

P

Perfect.

Q

But that I wasn't really interested in doing anything public –

P

So you'll play bad cop.

Q

Yes. Exactly. Now we can see how fuckin' bent these guys really are.

P *and* Q *both laugh.*

P

You know, between the three of 'em, they've written over two hundred scripts.

Q

I don't doubt it.

P

And all kinds of shit, too. All genres.

Q

I know, I know.

P

And the old guy! The old guy's written a four-hundred-pager called —

P *looks up, then stops. He lifts his elbows off the table.*

Q *looks back over his shoulder.*

P *stands up, extending his hand.*

P
(*to off-screen*)

Brian Tate, pleased to meet you.

Camera pans left.

As the camera pans left, A *'s hand reaches out to shake* P *'s hand. The hands meet up just as* P *'s body disappears and* A *'s smiling profile comes into view.*

The camera continues to pan left.

A
(*off-screen*)

And my name is...

TABLE ONE

Camera stops on B *and* C, *picking up their conversation in mid-sentence.*

C

... easily two of the best cinematic pornographers around today.
Easily. I mean, what these guys are doing – they're amazing. Sorta
like the Mitchell Brothers *Green Door*-era, but with smarts, right?
Really clever stuff. Good concept, good photography –

B

How many films have they made?

C
(*shrugs*)

I dunno. A dozen?

B

Which ones have you seen?

C

None. Just bits. Clips and stills mostly. I've read about their stuff,
though. Apparently Cronenberg's a big fan. He referred to them
when he was doing interviews for –

B

But you haven't *actually* seen any of their films.

C

Of course not. Nobody has. They did a couple of shorts back in the eighties, but other than that —

B

Nothing.

C

Right.

B

So how do you know they're any good?

C

They just are. You can tell. You can tell by the way they talk about their films.

B

Well, where have you heard them talk about their films? I mean, besides what Whitter —

C

Nowhere. I've just read bits here and there.

B

Where? I've never come across them in the trades.

C
(*scoffing*)

They're not *in* the trades.

B

Well...*where*, then?

C

Journals. They pop up in the journals.

B

Which ones?

C

Stuff you don't read. Like *Film Threat* and stuff.

B

I read *Film Threat*.

C

But not *Film Threat*, per se. French language stuff.

B

Oh. I don't read French.

C

No, you don't, do you?

B

No, I took Spanish in school.

C *takes a sip of beer and sighs deeply.* B *looks over his shoulder, then looks back at* C.

B

Whaddaya suppose they're talking about?

C

Same stuff as us.

B

Films, right?

C

Yup.

B *looks over his shoulder again, then looks back at* C.

B

The boss looks like he's doing most of the talking.

C

Of course. He's probably trying to pitch them on *A Nice Mentor*.

B

Have you actually read that thing?

C
(*knowingly*)

Oh yes.

B

Then you know there's no way it could ever be made into a film.

C

Yep. But that's what they said about *Naked Lunch*.

B

Well, yeah, but *Naked Lunch* wasn't a four-hundred-page screenplay.

C

Neither is *A Nice Mentor* anymore. I got it down to ninety pages.

B

What?!

C

Yeah, it was easy. I just made the camera the Nice Mentor. Plus I cut half the sex scenes.

B

So what the camera sees is what the Nice Mentor sees?

C

Basically.

B

Well, that's completely different from what the boss wrote. It's a completely different script now.

C

Exactly.

B

Did the boss approve the rewrites?

C

Nope.

B

Well, does he know that you even rewrote it?

C

Nope. And he isn't going to know, either.

B

He'll find out eventually. Then what are you gonna do?

C

He won't find out. There's no way. It's so different from the original he won't even recognize it.

c *takes a sip of his beer.*

I even changed the title.

B
(in horror)

To what?

C

O Mean Cretin.

A beat.

B

He's gonna kill you when he finds out.

C
(confidently)

No he's not.

c *takes another swig.*

Camera pans right.

TABLE TWO

p *and* q *are rapt.*

A
(in mid-sentence)

...so I figured once we got three hundred screenplays under our belt, then we'd start knockin' on doors.
(laughing)
I mean, the odds look pretty good that at least one of them's gonna get picked up, right?

q *nods, amused.*

P

Tell us about *A Nice Mentor.*

A
(proudly)

Ah, my baby.

98

P

Yeah.

A

I wrote that myself, you know.

A *throws a thumb over his shoulder.*

Long before those two bozos came on the scene.

P

Right. So what's it about?

A
(*coyly*)

Oh, about four hundred pages.

A *laughs, pushing the joke hard on* P *and* Q.

P *smiles politely.*

Q *cracks up, nudging* P *as if to say, «Can you believe this guy?»*

P

No, really. What's it about?

A *straightens up; his face gets serious. He takes a breath, then brings his elbows down on the table, clasping his hands together in an almost prayerful way. He sighs hard, then closes his eyes. He begins.*

A

A Nice Mentor is the story of a guidance counsellor at a youth detention centre on a small island off the coast of South Carolina. It opens with an overhead shot of the facility, then tracks in for a close-up: a man about thirty years old leaning on a railing overlooking the yard.

Q

He's the Nice Mentor.

P

Shh.

A
(*looking at* Q)

That's right. He's the Nice Mentor. And when I wrote this thing I had Redford in mind, but I guess he's a bit too old —

P

So what happens in the next three-hundred-and-ninety-nine pages?

A

Well, conditions at the centre are awful: overcrowding, bad food, gangs. The first two hours of the film builds up to a riot, then the riot, then the hostage taking. The Nice Mentor ends up being the negotiator.

P

How does it end?

A

War.

P

War between the inmates and the police.

A

No. War, as in Third World War. Just as the stand-off seems to be going nowhere, the United States is invaded by Commies. Then the inmates and police band together to hold off the invading horde.

P

At what point in the film does this happen?

A

The last half-hour.

P

Is there anything in the screenplay to suggest a tension between, say, the capitalist world and the communist world?

A

Oh yeah. But it's subtle. The detention centre's what you call a microcosm.

P

And when did you say you wrote this again?

A

Back in the seventies. But I looked at it the other day and it still holds up.

P

Well, don't you think that tensions between the capitalist world and the communist world are a bit...*passé*?

A

Sure. But that can be changed. We just make the commies Martians. Sorta the reverse of those sci-fi movies in the fifties.

P

Right.

Q

What about sex?

A

It's full of it. I've got shower scenes, work-out scenes, scenes between guards and inmates.

P

What about the Nice Mentor? Is there a love interest between him and....

Q
(*sardonically*)

Someone special?

A

Oh yeah. This is important. In the opening scene a bus comes through the gates and pulls up in the middle of the yard. And on the bus is this beautiful young boy. Let's just say he's the most beautiful boy in the world – blonde, thin. Anyway, the boy had been framed by one of the gangs in the centre, because they wanted to get him inside so they could make money pimping him to the other inmates. But he gets rescued by the Nice Mentor.

P

Okay.

Q

And where do the girls come from if this is an island detention centre for boys?

A *is shocked.*

A

There's no women in this film. It's about guys.

Q

Oh, so it's like a gay porno.

A
(*insulted*)
Absolutely not. This is a *very* serious film.

Q
But it's geared at the gay market?

A
No. This is a film for both men *and* women to enjoy.

Q
Yeah, but no hetero porn theatre is gonna show it. And no video store is gonna stock it outside the gay section.

A
Sure they will. Besides, this is an art film. This is gonna be up there with what's-his-name...Passonelli.

P
Pasolini.

A
Right. Him.

Q *realizes* A *is dead serious and proceeds to crack up.*

A *ignores him.*

P *gives* Q *a «knock-it-off» kinda look.* Q *tries to comply.*

P
I think you've got an interesting project here. I think if you just drop the communist invasion bit –

A
Martian.

P
Whatever. The Martian invasion bit. If you drop all that then I think you've got a pretty good story going. But four hundred pages?! Man, that's a lotta film.

A

Well, I need the invasion bit for the ending. You see, I'm trying to set it up for the sequel.

P

And what's that gonna be called?

A

Bitch Trains Emerge.

Q *cracks up again.*

P
(*chuckling*)

What's that one about?

A

It's an anagram for «The Germanic Tribes.» It's basically the story of how the world has been destroyed by Martians, and the detention centre is one of the last bastions of human civilization. That is, until some of the guys start smuggling women in. Anyway, these women are all hungry for men; but none of these guys want anything to do with them, 'cause all these woman want to do is have…

Camera pans right.

Q*'s laughter increases in volume, as* A*'s pitch trails off.*

TABLE THREE

HE

…and that's why I quit the theatre and applied to law school. Acting felt so shallow, so unsatisfying, so…*inconsequential.* Hey, I'll be honest: I wanna change the world. And the best way to do that, I think, is to make new law.

RAMÒN *begins to clap loudly.*

SHE *smiles at* RAMÒN, *then looks at* HER BROTHER.

HER BROTHER *scowls.*

> RAMÒN
> (*still clapping*)

Bravo! Bravo!

> HER BROTHER
> (*to* RAMÒN)

Alright, alright.

> (*turning to* HE)

Okay, Mr Smarty-Pants, so answer me this: what can you possibly do for a gay black man like myself who can't walk home at night for fear of having the shit kicked out of him? What law are you going to enact to ensure my safety?

> HE
> (*uncomfortably*)

Well – I mean – we all know assault-and-battery is a crime. But I know what you're getting at. How can we foster tolerance in a world created by white, heterosexual men? Well, that's an educational issue that –

> HER BROTHER

That you're just not able to answer. I mean, c'mon, you talk about tolerance – I don't wanna be just *tolerated*. I want respect. I want people to respect the fact that I am a black man. That I am a gay black man. And I just don't see that coming from lawyers. All you people do is send young black men to jail or defend old white fucks from tax evasion.

RAMÒN's *expression suggests the point is a good one.*

> HE

Hey, look. I don't claim to be the be-all-and-end-all of social justice. Your sister and I are just cogs in a big machine. We can't change attitudes overnight. We just wanna do our bit. So I'd appreciate it if you'd just –

HER BROTHER

Just what? Shut up? You want me to shut up? You can't handle
what I've got to say, so now you want me to shut up? Is that it? I
have no right to express my opinion? I've got no right to speak my
mind? To relate my experiences? D'ya know what you're doing
right now? D'ya know what this is all about?

HE *shrugs his shoulders, resigns himself to listen.*

HER BROTHER
(*looking around the table*)

I'll tell you what this is all about. It's about censorship, pure and
simple.

HER BROTHER *continues to look around the table; his expression is
pointed.*

HE, SHE, *and* RAMÒN *do their best to avoid eye contact.*

HE *takes a deep breath, then leans forward, elbows on the table.*

HE
(*sternly*)

Let me tell you something –

HER BROTHER
(*in mock astonishment*)

Tell me something?! You're gonna tell me something? Isn't that
what you've been doing all along? Telling me what to do, then
censoring my –

HE
(*loudly, angrily*)

Would you just shut up a minute!

SHE, HER BROTHER, *and* RAMÒN *jump back.*

HE
(*in a firm whisper*)

Let me tell you something right here, right now. I have not censored
you. I am in no way interested in censoring you. What you have to
say is important to me – far more important than you may think. I
am merely interested in having a polite conversation about...
(*searching*)
...*whatever* – anything.
(*turning to* RAMÒN)

I mean, Ramòn here asked me why I chose to study law. I don't
think it's unreasonable for me to answer him. Nor do I think it's
unreasonable for you to challenge my decision to enter the legal
profession. However, I do think it's unreasonable for you to
accuse me of censorship when all I was asking before you so
rudely attacked me was that you let me finish what I have to say
about –

HER BROTHER
(*snidely*)

Nothing. You have nothing to say about –

HE
(*agitated*)

You know, until you get that chip off your —

SHE
(*loudly*)

Enough! Enough of this bullshit! If you two can't along then I'm
outta here. And I mean it. I mean — *listen to yourselves!* Christ.
D'ya think Ramòn and I wanna spend our evening listening to
you two going on about...

(*to* HER BROTHER)

...censorship...

(*to* HE)

...and — *what* — polite society?

RAMÒN
(*raising his glass*)

I will drink to that!

SHE

I mean, you're both wrong, okay? Why don't we just leave it at
that.

SHE *leans back in her chair, frustrated, her arms crossed, not totally
content with the way she handled the matter.*

RAMÒN*'s eyes dart around the table. His smile is weak but hopeful.*

HE *and* HER BROTHER *face away from each other.*

SHE *composes herself, then, in an effort to make conversation...*

SHE
(*to* RAMÒN)

So, Ramòn, why don't you tell us more about your new place?

RAMÒN

Oh yes. Well. It is very, very nice. A corner suite. It looks right
over the market. You can see fruit stands and people singing and
playing instruments. And it is so big. Two bedrooms and dining
room and big kitchen and big, big living room, too. And the
floors — oh, the floors are all — how do you say? —

> HER BROTHER
> (*in a sulking tone*)

Hardwood.

> RAMÒN

Yes! Hardwood! And tile in the kitchen and bathroom that gets warm in the morning.

> SHE
> (*to* RAMÒN)

Wow, it must have cost you guys a fortune.

> HER BROTHER
> (*in a bragging tone*)

Nah, it was pretty reasonable – given the area. I managed to talk the agent down a couple of K and throw in an extra parking space.

HER BROTHER *takes in a self-satisfied breath.*

> Yep, she was pretty stingy, too. Didn't wanna budge. But I could tell they were having a hard time selling. I'd been watching those suites since they came on the market. Yeah, that agent. Typical Jew, ya know. Grind, grind, grind.

> HE

Sounds like you were the one doing the grinding.

> HER BROTHER
> (*insulted*)

Me? Are you kidding? Those suites were way overpriced to begin with. And you shoulda seen the way she looked at us when we walked in. It was like, Yeah, these guys aren't for real. They're just looky-loo faggots. No sale here. Fuck that. I showed her right.

SHE *shifts uncomfortably.*

HE *looks over at* SHE.

SHE *looks at* RAMÒN.

RAMÒN *shrugs.*

Camera pans right.

TABLE FOUR

The LIBERIAN *is standing between* W1 *and* W2. *He is completely naked.*

W2 *is sucking on his hard cock. Her right hand is alternating between his cock and testicles; her left hand is between her legs, making a small circular motion.*

W1 *is looking up at the Liberian, nodding along, attentive to what he is saying.*

LIBERIAN
(*to* W1)

It was difficult at first. Adjusting. Despite all the racism in America, I must say I was a little spoiled by the modern conveniences. Of course, when I first left for America, I had never seen a flush toilet before. But things began to change soon after I got home.

W1

For the better?

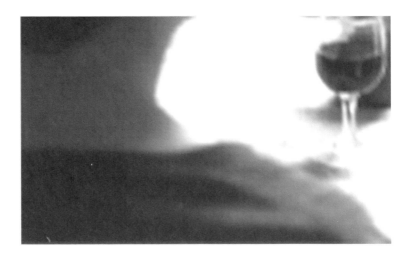

LIBERIAN

No, not at all. In fact, it was for the worse. Like America, my
village is now full of conveniences. And like America, my village
is now rife with racism, sexism, class-conflict. It is a very serious
problem.

w1 *looks confused.*

W1

All because of a few flush toilets?

LIBERIAN

It is much more complicated than that. In 1970 my village was
chosen as a test village – a village that was to be thoroughly modern-
ized – plumbing, electricity, central heating, television – then
studied by development agencies, anthropologists, multi-national
corporations, and so on. After ten years, our population went from
a hundred to twenty. Nobody in the village could stand it.

W1

They couldn't stand the scrutiny?

LIBERIAN

No, they couldn't stand the conveniences.

W1

How so?

LIBERIAN

Well, each convenience brought with it a different set of
problems. For instance, running water meant no more trips to
the well. So the children, whose task it had been to get up in the
morning and fetch water, were just getting up to watch television.
Another example had to do with food collection. In the old days,
we only took what we needed. But electricity made people lazy. It
destroyed our routines. So food collection went from a daily
activity to a monthly one. You see, the introduction of electricity
meant freezers. And freezers allow you to store food. So after the
children went to school for the day, the men would sit around and
watch American soap operas.

W 1

What about the women?

LIBERIAN

Well, the women ended up working harder. They spent all their time picking up after the men and the children. And that's were the problems began. The women revolted. They went on strike.

W 1

How did they do that?

LIBERIAN

They organized. Many of the woman had been attending evening classes. And one of the teachers, a university professor from San Francisco State, introduced the women to Marx and feminist critical theory. The women defined themselves as a trade union and called a strike.

W 1

Then what happened?

LIBERIAN

At first, they were ignored. The men forced the children to do all the garden work. But then the children revolted. Then the women began denying the men sex. Then it got *very* bad. The men began raping the women. And a lot of the women left. And they took the children with them. Then the men started to fight amongst themselves.

W 1

What were the police doing?

LIBERIAN

Nothing. They just stayed inside and watched TV.

W 1

That's awful.

LIBERIAN

Yes.

W1

What's your village like today?

LIBERIAN

The village today consists of a handful of men. All bad. Gangsters, really. Horrible men. Their business is custom refrigeration. People from outlying areas bring them meat and vegetables, which is processed and frozen for a fee. The whole town is basically one big butcher shop and cold storage.

W1

That's an awful story.

LIBERIAN

Yes, it is.

W1

But you're still there.

LIBERIAN

Yes.

W1

Why don't you leave?

LIBERIAN

I can't. I can't desert my village.

W1

But these people – they're terrible, terrible people.

LIBERIAN

Yes. But I am duty-bound. The village helped me become a doctor. And I am bound to stand by my village for as long as I am needed.

W1

But things have changed. Your village is obviously not the same village as the one that sent you to America.

LIBERIAN

Yes, but it is still my village.

w1 *makes a flabbergasted face. She is trying to say something, but nothing comes out.*

LIBERIAN

And what about you? You had big plans? Did you become a lawyer?

w1
(laughing)

Oh no. Not by a long shot. I didn't even finish my undergrad.

LIBERIAN

But you told me you wanted to become a lawyer. You spoke so passionately.

w1

I'm sure I did. But I got married instead. The winter after you left. To an accountant.

LIBERIAN

I thought all Americans got married in the spring?

w1

Not accountants. Accountants get married at the end of the year – for tax purposes.

LIBERIAN

Oh. I see.

w1

And pregnant women get married as soon as possible – at least where I came from.

He makes a confused face.

She laughs.

Then he laughs, too.

LIBERIAN

So you have at least one child?

W1

Two. A boy, Leonard, after his father. And a girl, Judith, after my ex-mother-in-law. They're both on their own now.

LIBERIAN

Are you on your own now, too?

W1

Well, yes. My husband ran off with his secretary about a year after Judith was born.

LIBERIAN

Oh. I'm sorry. Did you remarry?

W1

No. I spent all my time on the kids. And when they grew up I had to get a job. For the past few years I've been working as a legal secretary.

LIBERIAN

Do you like it?

W1

Oh yes. Very much. I love working. The lawyers I work for are idiots, but I get along well with the other secretaries.

LIBERIAN

Why don't you go back to school and become a lawyer yourself?

W1

Oh no. Not from what I've seen in the office.
(laughs)
I think the last thing I want to do is become one of them.

LIBERIAN

But there's so many different kinds of law. Surely you could find
something of interest out there. You told me in your letter that
you wanted to help people. What about –

W1

I know. But I'm too old for that now. I'd rather put my energies
into finding myself someone to spend the rest of my life with. A
companion.

(gazing off)

I think in a couple of years I'd like to sell my house and go on a
trip somewhere. You know, somewhere exotic. Like the
Caribbean or – I don't know – maybe Malta.

LIBERIAN

Malta is very close to Africa.

W1

Yes, I know.

The LIBERIAN smiles.

W1 smiles.

A beat.

W1

(snapping out of it)

But what about you? Did you get married? Did you have children?

LIBERIAN

Me?

(laughs)

No. No, I – my life – it was very difficult adjusting once I got back
from America. I spent a lot of time on my work. And I had
changed too much. For us, my people, marriage is something that
is very different than in America. I was – I became, as you say, out
of the loop.

W1

You must have been lonely.

LIBERIAN

Oh yes. I was. Very. But you just get used to it. You replacc it with other things.

W1

Like thoughts?

LIBERIAN

Pardon me?

W1

Thoughts. Fantasies.

LIBERIAN

Oh yes. Of course.

W1
(coyly)

Was I ever – you know – in your thoughts?

LIBERIAN

Yes, you were. Very much.

W1

You were in my thoughts, too.

LIBERIAN *nods, smiles.*

W1 *smiles back.*

W2 *takes her mouth off the Liberian's cock, leans back in her chair, and orgasms.*

Camera pans left.

TABLE THREE

HE, SHE, *and* RAMÒN *are listening.*

HER BROTHER
(*boastfully, in mid-sentence*)

...and that if I wasn't gonna get an interview, then I was outta there. Period.

SHE

But it sounds like you were gonna get an interview, anyway. Why make a big fuss about something that was already coming your way?

HER BROTHER

You can't take anything for granted with this company. I mean, when I started there five years ago, in the mail room, there was this guy, this black guy, real smart, you know, knew everything about the business – and he had been in the mail room for six years! *Six years!* And this guy was ambitious! But he had no confidence. He never spoke up. So, when positions were posted, he'd just drop off his resumé, you know. He never followed up. Never got an interview. That's why he's still in the mail room. A complete waste of talent, if you ask me.

SHE

Well, you're management now. You've got, what, twenty people under you? Why don't you hire him?

HER BROTHER

Are you kidding? The guy's got no initiative. He's proved that already. Why would I want somebody like that under me? I want somebody whose gonna go out there and grab the tiger by the tail.

HE

Like you.

HER BROTHER

Exactly. Like me. Only not as smart as me.

SHE

Well, why is he still with the company if he can't get out of the mail room?

HER BROTHER
(*shrugs*)

Beats me. I haven't talked to the guy since I moved up to sales.

SHE

I guess things are pretty compartmentalized over there. I guess when you leave one department it's like moving to another city.

HER BROTHER
(*shaking his head*)

Not at all. The offices are all pretty open. That guy from the mail room – I see him every day. He hands me my mail.

HE

And you never talk?

HER BROTHER

Nope. I've got nothing to say to him. I mean, he tries to engage me in stuff – news, weather, sports – you know, small-talk stuff. But I don't bite. I know he's just trying to loosen me up, trying to get me to offer him something. But I don't want no suck-hole hangin' around me.

SHE

Well, maybe he's just trying to make conversation? Maybe he considers you a friend from all that time you spent working together?

HER BROTHER

Why would he consider me a friend? We just worked together, that's all.

SHE

Maybe he doesn't see it that way.

HER BROTHER
(*shrugs*)

Maybe.

SHE

Maybe if you said something to him, though. What if you told him
to be a bit more assertive?

HER BROTHER

Nah, he's not that kinda guy. He just doesn't have it, ya know.
Besides that's not my job.

HE

Well, doesn't your company sponsor courses in that kinda stuff?
It wouldn't hurt to encourage him to look into something like
that, would it?

HER BROTHER
(*suspiciously*)

Look, why are you guys taking such an interest in this loser? It
ain't worth it, believe me. He's just not worth it.
(*lightening up*)
Man, it's sure not hard to tell you guys are lawyers – always
picking away at the details. Get outta here! You're drivin' me nuts.

HE

But really, though. I mean, you said it yourself: this guy knows all
this stuff about the business. And the only way you could've
known that is by him telling you what he knows. And surely you
must've benefited from all that knowledge. Surely that would've
helped you negotiate your way up the company ladder. So don't
you think you owe him something for all that –

HER BROTHER
(*pissed off*)

I owe him nothing! The guy's a fuckin' loser, okay?! If he ain't
smart enough to keep his mouth shut, then he ain't smart enough
to get ahead in the company. Knowledge is power. This guy was
givin' it away! And I'm smart enough to take it. So don't try and
lecture me on something you know dick-all about. And don't try
and lay that kindness-to-neighbours bullshit on me, boy. That's
not the way it works in business. I'm way ahead of you on this
one. Way ahead.

HE *shakes his head, then looks over at* SHE.

SHE *puts a hand up to her face, as if to hide her embarrassment.*

EXTREME CLOSE-UP ON HER WRIST-WATCH

The time is 7:24.

HE *looks like he's just remembered something.*

                    HE
                (standing up)
    'Scuse me.

HE *leaves quickly.*

SHE *watches him leave, confused.*

                HER BROTHER
                (to SHE)
    I mean, look at Ramòn over there. Just yesterday he was telling
    me about some kid at the gym, a real nice kid, everybody likes
    him — Jesse. Was that his name, Ramòn? Jesse?

RAMÒN *nods.*

> HER BROTHER

Whatever. Anyway, this Jesse's a real knock-out puncher. Right-hander with a killer left hook. Great legs. Smart boxer. But he lacks one thing.

HER BROTHER *cocks an eyebrow, as if to solicit guesses.*

SHE *shrugs.*

> He lacks the killer instinct. He lacks desire. So what do you do with that? What trainer is gonna get involved with that? What manager is gonna get behind some kid with great tools who doesn't want to fight? And as much as the other boxers like him, respect him, what fighter is gonna let this guy walk all over them? Ya see what I'm getting at? It's not enough to have the tools, you gotta deliver. You gotta want to –

Two policemen enter the frame, one on either side of RAMÒN.

POLICEMAN 1 *is black,* POLICEMAN 2 *is white.*

SHE'S *startled, confused.*

> HER BROTHER
> (*his back up*)

What the fuck's goin' on here?

> SHE
> (*to* HER BROTHER)

Don't say anything.

> POLICEMAN 1
> (*to* RAMÒN)

Are you Ramòn Javier Rodriguez?

> RAMÒN

Yes.

> POLICEMAN 1

Mr Rodriguez, you're under arrest for the murder of Jesse Allen Douglas. You have the right...

POLICEMAN 2 *makes an «on your feet» gesture to* RAMÒN.

RAMÒN *complies.*

> HER BROTHER
>
> What the *fuck's* goin' on?

> SHE
> (*to* HER BROTHER)
>
> Shut up! Don't say anything!

> POLICEMAN 1
> (*continuing*)
>
> ...to remain silent. Anything you say or do can and will be used against you in a court of law. You have the right...

> HER BROTHER
>
> This is bullshit! He's done nothing —

> POLICEMAN 2
>
> Listen to your girlfriend, pal.

POLICEMAN 1 *cuffs* RAMÒN, *then swings him around, out of frame.*

> HER BROTHER
> (*jumping up*)
>
> We have attorneys right here, and we're not gonna take this bullshit police harassment. My friend here has done nothing wrong. This is police-fuckin'-harassment. Pure and simple. Why aren't you guys out bustin' white-collar —

POLICEMAN 2 *pokes* HER BROTHER *hard on the sternum with his finger, knocking him back in his chair.*

HER BROTHER *makes a half-hearted attempt at lunging from the chair, then, upset, resigns himself to what's happening.*

> POLICEMAN 2
> (*to* HER BROTHER)
>
> Look, buddy, you are two inches away from obstruction. Sit down and shut the fuck up or you're gonna be goin' downtown with Mr Rodriguez here.

POLICEMAN 2 *glances over his shoulder.*
> (*to* POLICEMAN 1)
> You okay to call it in?

> POLICEMAN 1
> (*off screen*)
> Yeah.

POLICEMAN 2 *pulls out a notepad and pen.*

> POLICEMAN 2
> (*to* HER BROTHER)
> Did you say you were an attorney? Mr Rodriguez's attorney?

> SHE
> (*to* HER BROTHER, *sternly*)
> You don't have to answer that. You don't have to say anything.

> HER BROTHER
> (*gesturing with his thumb*)
> No, *she's* the attorney.
> (*to* SHE, *in a scared whisper*)
> Do something, girl.

POLICEMAN 2 *looks at* SHE.

> SHE
> (*flustered*)
> Uh, no, officer. I'm not an attorney – yet. I'm, uh – I work for the District Attorney's office, but I haven't, uh – I never said I was an attorney, though. Uh, my brother –

HE *enters the frame, looking around, confused.*

> HE
> What's going on?

HER BROTHER *turns his head towards* HE, *then double-takes. His expression is almost revelatory, as if he has just put two-and-two together.*

POLICEMAN 2 *continues to write on his pad.*

POLICEMAN 2
(*to* SHE)

Can I have your full name, please, ma'am?

SHE

Uh, I never said I was an attorney. I just want to make that clear, okay?

HE

Would somebody please tell me what's going on here?
(*looking around*)

Where's Ramòn?

HER BROTHER'*s eyes squinch up, as he slowly rises from his chair.*

HER BROTHER
(*to* HE)

You! You fucking *puke!* You — you phoned the fucking cops, didn't you?

HE

I don't know what you're talking about.

SHE *looks at* HER BROTHER, *then at* HE. SHE *does this twice.* SHE *doesn't know what to believe.*

HER BROTHER *looks down at the table and grabs a glass, letting go with everything he's got, in the direction of* HE.

HE *ducks, the glass smashes against the wall.*

POLICEMAN 2 *lunges at* HER BROTHER, *wrestling him to the floor.*

HER BROTHER *is screaming obscenities.*

SHE *gets up from her chair, her face panic-stricken.*

POLICEMAN 2 *gets* HER BROTHER *to his feet, throws him over the table, then pulls out his handcuffs.*

> POLICEMAN 2
>
> Okay, buster. You're goin' downtown.

> SHE
>
> I'm sorry, officer. He's my brother. He's just a bit upset, that's all.

POLICEMAN 2 *cuffs* HER BROTHER, *while* HER BROTHER *just lays there, motionless, sobbing.*

POLICEMAN 2 *looks up at* HE.

> POLICEMAN 2
> (*to* HE)
>
> Do you wanna press charges?

HE *just stands there, stunned.*

> HE
>
> Uh, no. No, it's alright.

> POLICEMAN 2
> (*to* SHE)
>
> I'm gonna have to take your brother downtown, ma'am. Are you okay with that?

SHE
(*dumfounded*)

Uh, am I okay with that? Whaddaya mean *am I okay with that*?

POLICEMAN 2 *pulls out his walkie-talkie and calls for back up, then he pulls* HER BROTHER *hard off the table, spinning him around.*

HE *and* SHE *stand together, watching in disbelief.*

The camera follows POLICEMAN 2, *as he escorts* HER BROTHER *past Table Two.*

TABLE TWO

P, Q, B, *and* C *watch as the cop and* HER BROTHER *exit, camera-left.*

B

Wow.

Q
(*turning back to the table, excited*)

I don't think I've ever seen anyone arrested for murder before.

B

Me neither.

C
(*to* P)

What about you? Ever seen someone get arrested for murder?

P
(*shaking his head*)

Nope. You?

C
(*to* P)

Ever seen someone get murdered before?

P
(*shaking his head*)

Nope.

C
(*slyly*)

Really?

P

Yep. Really.

C
(*to* Q)

What about you? You ever seen someone get murdered before?

Q *eyes dart over to* P *and back.*

Q

No.

C *looks back at* P, *then to* Q *again.* C *does this twice. He takes a breath, smiling on the exhale. Then:*

C

What about *Factory Girl*?

Q *looks nervously at* P.

P *stays cool.*

B

What's *Factory Girl*?

B *is ignored.*

P

What about it?

C

Well, was it faked?

Q
(*looking around*)

Was what faked?

C
(laughing)

C'mon, you know what I'm talking about. *Factory Girl*. Was the scene faked or what?

P

Are you saying that you've seen *Factory Girl*?

B

What's *Factory Girl*?

C
(to P)

Yes.

P

When and where did you see it?

C

I can't say where. But I saw it about five years ago.

P

Did you see it in Vegas? At Consumer Electronics?

C

I can't say.

P

Are you saying you can't say because you're not allowed to tell anyone? Or are you saying you can't say because you never really saw it?

B
(to Q)

What are they talking about?

Q

Nevermind.

C
(grinning)

No, I saw it alright.

(*pause*)

But did *you* make it?

P

You are venturing into some very dangerous territory here.

C

No, I think it is *you* that is venturing into the dangerous territory.

B

Could somebody please tell me what's going on here? And what the fuck is *Factory Girl*?

Q *looks nervously at* P.

P *leans over and whispers something into* Q*'s ear.*

C

No secrets, guys.

B *is confused. His eyes dart around the table.*

C
(*leaning forward*)

Look, we've told you about some of our projects. The least you could do is tell us about some of yours.

B
(*firmly*)

Yeah. And I wanna know about *Factory Girl*.

Q

Forget it. It ain't gonna happen.

P

It's nothing personal. It's just that we don't know who you are.

Q

Yeah, you guys could be cops for all we know.

C

But we're not. And you know it.

B
(*to* C)

Maybe *they're* cops.

C

Or maybe they're just garbagemen — like us.

B *snickers.*

P *is still playing it cool.*

Q *'s forehead is beginning to bead.*

C

So how 'bout it, guys? Did you fake that scene or what?

B *stares at* P. B *doesn't know what's going on, but he's rapt in anticipation.*

Q *stares at* P. *A drop of sweat runs down* Q*'s brow.*

P *pulls a cigarette out of his pack, lights it, puts the lighter down, exhaling, all the while staring at* C.

P

We never made a film called *Factory Girl*.

B *looks confused.*

Q *wipes his brow.*

C *nods, smiles.*

C

I know. I just made it up. I just wanted to see if you two were full of shit.

P *smiles.*

P

And now you know.

C

That's right. And now we know.

Camera pans left.

TABLE ONE

Table One is empty. THE BARTENDER *is picking up empty beer bottles with one hand, dumping ashtrays into a coffee can with the other. He is humming something of his own invention. The camera lingers for a minute, then continues left.*

TABLE FOUR

W1 *and* W2 *sit quietly, as people often do once they've run out of stuff to talk about. They look very much like they did when we first came upon them.*

W1 *is smoking.*

W2

So?

W1 *realizes she's being talked to, then jerks to attention.*

W1
(*startled*)

What was that, dear?

W2
(*nods towards w1's empty glass*)

Are you gonna have another drink?

W1

What time is it?

W2
(*looking at her watch*)

About seven-thirty.

W1

One more.

W2

Me too.

w1 *looks towards the bar, raises her hand in a peace sign, then makes a revolving gesture. She mouths the word «two,» then lowers her hand.*

w2 *lights a cigarette.*

W1

Are you still seeing that guy?

W2
(*exhaling, laughing*)

God no. You mean Peter, right?

W1

Yeah.

W2

No.
(*finishing her drink*)

That wasn't a real thing. I don't know what I was thinking with that one. He was just around, ya know?

W1

Hmm. It was pretty serious last Friday.

W2

Yeah, until he fucked up.

W1

How so?

W2

Aw, we were supposed to go out for dinner or something – a date, right? And he just – the fuckin' guy phones an hour after he was supposed to pick me up and says he's too tired. And I'm like – there's all this loud music and people talking in the background and he's got this put-on sleepy voice going. And I'm like – fuck this. So I just hung up on him.

W1
(putting out her cigarette)

Men can be the biggest idiots.

W2
(slightly upset)

No fuckin' kidding.

W1 notices the quiver in W2's voice. She cocks her head sympathetically.

W1

Hey, it's okay. At least you're not married to him.

W2

I guess.

W1

My, uh, ex-husband, he used to do that to me all the time. He'd be at his secretary's house and he'd phone to tell me he was still at the office, working late. And I could hear the sound of a shower running in the background.

They both laugh.

W1

Yeah, after a while I'd just slough it off. It was all so stupid.

W2
(*cheering up*)

Did he really? Did he really do that, though?

W1

Oh yeah. He was the worst liar.

W2

Did you ever have affairs on him?

W1

Are you kidding? Where would I have the time? Between the two kids and running a household – and volunteering for everything that had a whale in its logo – I didn't have a minute to myself for twenty years. And it got busier after he left. Having to be the dad, as well. The dad he never was.

W1 *kills the last of her drink.*

He didn't even visit the kids for two years. Didn't want to see 'em, he said. Can you imagine that?

W2
(*shrugs*)

I guess having kids is a lot of work, huh?

W1
(*smiling*)

Oh yeah. But they're worth it. They're good kids. I don't see them that much, but they're good kids.

W2

So what about now? Are you seeing anyone?

W1

Nah, I haven't –
(*tilting her head, thinking*)
I think it's been, what, twenty-some years since he left? Yeah, and I haven't been with a man since. No regrets.

W 2

Really?

W 1

Yep.

W 2

Don't you get lonely?

W 1

Oh sure. Sometimes. But I fill my time up pretty good. I've got work and friends and volunteering —

W 2

Yeah, but don't you get lonely for sex?

W 1
(*laughing*)
I've got my vibrator. *And* my imagination.

W 2
(*seriously*)
Well, yeah, but don't you miss the real thing?

W 1

Honey, the real thing is running out of batteries at two o'clock in the morning. Besides, most of the men I've met are nightmares. And why have nightmares when you can have daydreams? That's what I always say.

W 2 *butts out her cigarette.*

W 1 *leans towards her.*

W 1

Hey, if I can give you a little piece of advice: get it out of your head that it takes a man to make you happy. Once you do that you'll be laughing.

W2

Yeah, but I like men. And I like having sex with them. But the thought of being involved with one man for the rest of my life kinda freaks me out. And I definitely don't want to be saddled with kids. No offence or anything.

W1

None taken.

W1 *lights a cigarette, takes a drag, blows the smoke out her nose.*

W2

Yeah, it's like what you said earlier, about how the sixties are seen as revolutionary; but that they were still, at the same time, really conservative.

W1 *makes an understanding face.*

W1

Well, what I meant was –

W2
(*interrupting*)

Yeah. It's like, in a lotta ways, nothing has changed, right? It's more like things have just been rearranged. That's the way I see it. I remember my high school guidance teacher telling us that it was alright for women – in fact, it was expected of women – to pursue careers, that they shouldn't have to be housewives and mothers if they didn't want to. But there's still so many things in society that tell us to stay at home.

W1

That's right.

W2

But what they never told us about was what we could do or where we could go when, you know, our families started to put pressure on us to get married and settle down and have kids and all that. And that stuff, to me, is, like, way more important than anything else. The support, right?

W1

Right.

W2

I mean, look at me. I'm an only child. And both my parents come
from large families. And all my aunts and uncles have tons of kids
– and tons of grandkids. For the past few years my parents have
been on my back constantly about making them grandparents.
But I don't want that. And I definitely don't want to get married.

W1

Have you told them this?

W2

Oh yeah. It comes up all the time. They treat it like it's a big deal.
And then when I get pissed off, they lay this guilt trip on me: *Oh,
all our brothers and sisters have grandkids and we feel left out and it
makes us feel like there's something wrong with us.* And then they
turn it around, like I've got something wrong with *me*.

W1 *shakes her head in sympathy.*

The bartender gives them their drinks.

W2 *picks up her glass and downs half of it.*

W2

I mean – three years ago I got pregnant. I dated this guy from the
IRS. Remember him? Rick? He was around during the audit?

W1 *thinks hard for a second, then nods.*

w2

Anyway, I dated him three times, then had sex with him on the third date. Nice guy. Boring, but nice. And he seemed safe, right? I mean, he'd just broken up with his wife and he made it clear he just wanted to have some fun – no strings. So we went out. He had tickets to something – some musical. Anyway, we got back to his place around one in the morning. And it was like, Why not? So we start necking. And one thing led to another, and we ended up in the bedroom. Well, we were both a little tipsy by then, and he was having problems with the condom, so I just let him in, right? And that was it. A few weeks later I found out I was pregnant.

w2 *downs the rest of her drink.*

w1 *takes a little sip.*

w1

You had an abortion?

w2

No.

w2 *takes a hard look at* w1, *inviting her to guess again.*

w1
(*shrugs*)

You miscarried?

w2 *shakes her head.*

w1
(*laughing nervously*)
You didn't have the baby. I think I would've noticed that.

w2 *'s eyes well up.*

w1
(*compassionately*)

Oh dear. What happened?

w2 *wipes her eyes, then hardens up again.*

W 2

Well, I went home for Sunday dinner – the Sunday after I found out. And my parents began their usual harangue about grandkids. So – I don't know what I was thinking – I just told them. I said I was pregnant. I mean, I hadn't even thought about what I was gonna do with it or anything. I just blurted it out. I said, «Well, I just went to see Doctor Wertz and he told me I was pregnant and the baby's due in the spring.» And it felt great.

w2 begins to slow down, her voice shaky.

For a brief second it felt really, really great, ya know? I felt really warm inside, like this big geyser just – you know? And I smiled and I waited for them to smile or – I don't know – do *something*, right? And they just sat there. Staring. And then my father's face just kinda twisted into this awful knot. And then the next thing I knew I was on my ass and my father was on top of me just wailing away. And I was calling out for my mother and all I could hear were her footsteps running down the hall and the bedroom door slamming and that was it. My father beat the shit out of me and about an hour later my mother drove me home.

w1 reaches out to take w2's hand.

W 1
(softly)

I'm so sorry.

w2 takes a cocktail napkin, wipes her eyes, then blows her nose.

A beat.

W 2

You remember that trampoline accident I had?

w1 nods slowly.

W 2

Well…it wasn't an accident.

w1 smiles sadly.

W2

I've never been on a trampoline in my life.

w2 *breaks down.*

w1 *comforts her.*

Camera pans left.

TABLE THREE

HE *and* SHE *are in the original positions.*

HE *is crouched over his cellphone, getting nowhere with whoever's on the line.*

SHE *is staring at him. Her expressions range from shock to anticipation, despair to rage.*

HE

Whaddaya mean he left town? He didn't tell me he left town. He —

HE *listens, then shakes his head.* HE *looks over at* SHE.

SHE *looks away, biting her lip.*

HE
(*to* SHE)

D'ya have a pen?

SHE *starts digging in her purse.*

HE *takes the coaster from the ashtray and unfolds it, turning it over, gum side down.*

SHE *hands him the pen.*

HE *writes something down on the coaster.*

HE

555-2721. Got it. And if you hear from Rupert, tell him I can be reached on my cell? 555-8830. Yeah. Great. Thanks, Janey. Thanks a lot.

HE *puts the cellphone down on the table, then lets out a sigh.*

SHE

What? What's happening?

HE

If we don't hear from Rupert in ten minutes, then we can phone him at home.
(*sighing again*)
We owe Janey big time.

SHE

I can't believe this. I just can't believe this is happening. Can't we go down to the station? Isn't there something we can do?

HE

No. Janey said to sit tight until we hear from Rupert.

SHE

I don't see why we can't we go down there and wait.

HE

No. There's no point. There's nothing we can do. We're not lawyers — yet.

SHE
(*pleading*)
Yeah, but he's my brother, for chrissake!

HE

I know, I know. But they won't let you see him, anyway.

SHE *picks up the coaster, rolls it around in her hand, then tosses it down.*

HE *turns around and waves for the bartender, nodding as if the bartender gestured «Two more.»*

SHE

I can't believe they think Ramòn killed somebody. He's so... harmless.

HE

Harmless? He's a boxer, for fuck's sake.

SHE

Well, that doesn't mean he's a killer.

HE

No, but it doesn't make him harmless, either.

SHE

Shit, I hope my brother isn't involved in this. Oh god, when my mom finds out she's gonna –

HE

Forget it. Forget even thinking like that. We don't even know Ramòn's involved. Who knows – maybe the cops are bluffing?

SHE

Then we should go down there and talk to them.

HE

No, we've made a plan and we're gonna stick with it.

SHE
(*crossing her arms*)
This doesn't feel right, sitting here.

HE
I don't care if it doesn't feel right. We've got a plan in motion and we've agreed to it with Janey and we're not gonna fuck it up.

SHE
(*to herself*)
Shit.

HE *picks up the coaster, plays with it. He is deep in thought.*

SHE *reaches into her purse and pulls out a package of gum.*

HE
What do you know about Ramòn, anyway?

SHE
(*shaking her head slowly*)
Not much. I met him once before. That was before he and my brother were officially a couple. And, I dunno, he seemed pleasant. He didn't say much. He's a middleweight contender. That's about all I know.

HE
Hmm.

SHE
Why?

HE
(*staring at his hands as they fidget with the coaster*)
No reason.

A beat.

SHE
You're hiding something. You know something, don't you?

HE
(*eyes on the coaster*)

What are you talking about?

SHE

I saw the way you looked at Ramòn when he walked in. You recognized him, didn't you? You know him from somewhere?

HE
(*looking off*)

I don't know what you're talking about.

SHE *sighs, incredulous, leaning back hard in her chair.*

HE *looks at her.*

HE

Okay, he did look familiar. He looked like somebody I knew from theatre school. But that was years ago.

SHE *jumps up from her slump.*

SHE
(*quickly*)

Who? What was his name?

HE
(*uncomfortably*)

What difference does it make? You wouldn't know him, anyway.

SHE

Okay, then. Who did you phone when you got up from the table?

HE
(*defensively*)

I told you. I phoned Tulane's. From a payphone.

SHE

Why didn't you use your cell?

HE

Probably for the same reason you used the payphone when you called your brother. Privacy. Plus I wanted it to be a surprise.

HE *leans back from the table.* HE *looks hurt.*

What are you getting at, anyway? Do you think I phoned the cops? Do you think I brought the cops here?

SHE *grabs the cellphone.*

HE
(*nervously*)

What are you doing?

SHE *ignores him.*

HE *leans forward, extending his hand.*

HE

C'mon, gimme that. Rupert might be trying to get through.

SHE
(*leaning away from him*)

Yes, operator, I'd like the number of Tulane's Restaurant.

HE *stretches his arm out a little more, gesturing for the phone with his fingers.*

HE

C'mon. Don't tie up the line.

SHE

Thank you, operator.

SHE *pulls away from him and begins to dial the number to Tulane's.*

HE *lunges over and grabs the phone, turning it off.*

HE

Look, if you think I'm full of shit, then you can just fuck off.

SHE *grabs her purse and stands up to leave.*

The cellphone rings.

SHE *freezes.*

> HE
> (*answering the phone*)
>
> Hello…Rupert!

HE *listens intently for a few seconds, then looks at* SHE.

> HE
>
> Great. Janey did a good job briefing you. Yeah, we're at a bar up
> on −

SHE *grabs the phone from* HE.

> SHE
> (*backing away from* HE)
>
> Rupert?…Yeah, it's me. Sorry for interrupting, but did you hear
> about Ramòn from Janey first or did −

> HE
> (*standing up, angrily*)
>
> What the fuck do you think you're doing?

> SHE
>
> Because it's important that I know, Rupert. It's −

HE *moves toward her, his hand outstretched.*

SHE *moves back.*

> SHE
> (*upset*)
>
> Why can't you tell me?

> HE
> (*angrily*)
>
> Give me the fuckin' phone, bitch.

SHE *continues to step backwards, away from* HE.

The other tables are now in view. But they are empty.

SHE
(*frightened*)
Rupert! RUPERT, PLEASE!

HE *grabs at the phone, trying to wrestle it from her hands.* SHE *puts up a fight.*

SHE
(*desperately*)
Rupert!...Rupert! Just tell me. *Please.*

The phone falls, but HE *ignores it.* HE *strikes* SHE *with his open hand under her chin.*

SHE
(*terrified*)
WHAT ARE YOU DOING?! GET AWAY FROM ME!

HE *strikes her again, with his fist, opening a cut above her right eye.*

SHE *reaches down to pick up the phone.*

HE *kicks her hard in the stomach, lifting her completely off the ground.*

SHE *falls to the floor, doubled over.*

HE *continues to kick her.*

HE *seems oblivious to what he's doing, as if something has rolled in front of him and he's kicking it out of the way.*

SHE *covers her face...*

SHE
OH, MY GOD! SOMEBODY HELP! HELP ME! OH, GOD!
SOMEBODY HELP ME, PLEASE!

HE *kicks her again.*

SHE *screams.*

And again.

SHE *screams.*

And again.

Camera pans right.

Screams fade.

TABLE FOUR

w1 *holds* w2 *in her arms.* w2 *is sobbing heavily.* w1 *is humming a tune, a lullaby.*

Camera pans right.

TABLE ONE

A *comes running towards Table One carrying a huge, messy stack of typed pages. He dumps the pages onto the vacant table, where they spill loose. He stands there smiling, like he's just won the lottery.*

A
(to Table Two)

Here it is, guys. *A Nice Mentor*.

Camera pans right.

TABLE TWO

P, Q, B, *and* C *remain in their seats.*

P *and* Q *look at each other. This time they look nervous.*

C *smiles slyly at both of them.*

All you can hear is the rustle of pages from Table One.

B
(to A*)*

Hey, boss, you missed the action. Some guy at the next table just got arrested for murder.

A
(*off-screen*)

Yeah, whatever. The spook probably had it coming.

B

Nah, it wasn't the spook. It was the spic.

P and Q look at each other.

They look scared.

C
(*to P and Q*)

Yeah, but they took the spook with them.

A
(*off-screen*)

Now that's what I call killing two birds with one stone.

B laughs, then looks over at C.

C cracks a grin.

Camera pans left.

TABLE ONE

A is smiling. He claps his hands together, hard, then wrings them.

A

Okay, boys, get over here. We're gonna do a cold reading for Mr Whitter and Mr Tate. And maybe – just maybe – they're gonna like what they hear so much they'll get their friend the Baron to finance *A Nice Mentor*.

We hear the scuff of chairs and the shuffling of feet.

B and C enter the frame at camera-right. They take up their original places: B camera-right, C camera-left, A in the middle.

P and Q enter the frame once B and C sit down.

A

(*to* P *and* Q)

Over here, beside me. One on either side.

B *and* C, *still in their chairs, scoot over, making room.*

Q *is petrified.*

P *walks out of frame, then re-enters with two chairs.*

P *puts a chair between* A *and* B, *then puts a chair between* A *and* C.

P *sits down on the chair between* A *and* C.

Q *continues to stand.*

A

(*to* Q)

Come on now. We don't have all night.

A *begins sorting through the manuscript.*

Q, *shaking like crazy, sits down.*

A *pulls out ten sheets of paper from the middle of the pile. He divides them into three piles, giving one pile to* B *and one pile to* C. *He straightens the third pile and lays it in front of himself.*

A

(*putting on his glasses*)

Okay, we're gonna do the first love scene between A Nice Mentor and the boy, Bobby.

(*from the page*)

Bobby's just been gang raped by the Cretin gang and he's lying on the floor of the shower room sobbing. A Nice Mentor hears the sobs and follows them. He finds Bobby curled up beneath a running shower. He walks over and turns off the steaming shower, then bends down and places his hand on the boy's shoulder.

(*to* B)

You are Bobby.

(*to* c)

You are Dr Carl.

(*looking around the table*)

And I'm A Nice Mentor.

A beat.

Action.

B *lowers his head and pretends to sob.*

A *looks at* B.

B *laughs, then exaggerates the sobbing noises.*

A
(*from the page*)

A Nice Mentor softly rubs the back of Bobby's neck.

There, there, little one. It's okay. Everything's gonna be just fine.

B
(*from the page, pretending to whimper*)

Please. Please don't touch me. Please. No.

A
(*from the page*)

I'm not gonna hurt you, little one. It's okay. It's just me. A Nice Mentor.

B
(*lifting his head*)

A Nice Mentor? Is it really you?

A

Bobby looks up and smiles. He touches his hand to A Nice Mentor's face.

A beat.

A *throws a hard look at* B.

B *looks uncomfortable. Reluctantly he touches* A*'s face, then looks back to his text.*

B
(from the page)

Oh thank god. You've come to save me.

A *looks up from his script, looking at* B.

A

Yes, Bobby. And I'm gonna make sure nothing like this ever
happens again.

B
(from the page)

Ohhh.

A *continues to look at* B. *He gently pushes his lines aside, for he knows this
script by heart.*

A

Bobby tries to put his hands around A Nice Mentor's neck, then
falls down, rolling over on his back. A Nice Mentor begins to
gently rub Bobby's genitals, singing to him a song that goes like
this:

(*singing, in a warbly falsetto*)

I am like the hand-hold of the shepherd of the lamb

Putting little boys to sleep with a sprinkling of sand

They sleep so tight in my palm through the night

And they wake happily in the yellow morning light

I am like the kiss of —

C
(*from the page, in a bored monotone*)

I heard singing.

A

Ah, Dr Carl. I was singing to young Bobby here. He's been assaulted. Brutally raped.

C
(*from the page, same monotone*)

Oh my god, A Nice Mentor.

A

Yes, I'm trying to ease his pain.

C
(*from the page, monotone*)

Good work. Let me look at his rectum. There might some tearing.

A

Dr Carl spreads Bobby's legs and examines his rectum.

C
(*from the page, monotone*)

Hmm. You're right, A Nice Mentor. This is serious. Young Bobby may never have sexual intercourse again.

A
(*melodramatically, throwing up his arms*)

OH, LORD IN HEAVEN!

Q
(*loudly interrupting*)
Ah, great stuff, guys. Listen, we've gotta get going now…
(*rising, glancing at his watch*)
…so if you guys would just give us your names and numbers we'll –

A
(*angrily*)
Hey! Sit the fuck down! We're not finished yet.

P
Uh, sorry, but we are.
(*waving towards the bar*)
Tab, please.

A *grabs* P *by the wrist and slams it down on the table, holding it there.*

A
(*mocking* P)
Uh, sorry, but we *aren't.*

A*'s smile is positively sinister.*

P *looks down, his wrist being ground into a broken ashtray. Blood is pooling.*

A *eases off.*

P *slowly withdraws his bloody hand.*

A
(*rising, to* B *and* C)
Watch 'em.

A *exits towards the bar.*

A
(*off-screen*)
Hey, I'll take care of that. How much do I owe ya?

P *and* Q *are terrified: their complexions are white.*

C *tosses a couple of cocktail napkins at* P.

P *applies the napkins to his bleeding wrist.*

C
(*to* P *and* Q)
You guys wanna get outta here?

Q *nods his head quickly.*

P *grimaces in pain.*

C *looks over his shoulder, towards the bar, then back at* P *and* Q.

A's *laugh can be heard off-screen. He's in the middle of telling a joke.*

C
I'll get you outta here. But it's gonna cost you, okay?

Q
Yeah, yeah. Fine. Whatever.

C
You're prepared to make a deal?

P
Yeah.

Q
Yeah. Anything.

C *looks over his shoulder again, towards the bar, then back at* P *and* Q.

A's *still telling his joke.*

C *reaches into his pocket and pulls out his keys.*

C
(*to* B)
Bring my car around front. When these two come out, take them back to my place and wait for me there. If they give you any trouble, there's a gun under the seat.

B
Okay.

c *passes* b *his keys.*

b *gets up and goes.*

A beat.

C

Now who are you?

p *looks over at* q.

Q

We're not Whitter and Tate.

C

No kidding. So who the fuck are you?

Q

My name is –

P

I'm a cop.
(tilting his head towards q)
And he works for the District Attorney's Office.

q *throws* p *a startled look.*

C
(to q)

Bet you never thought he'd blow your cover like that, did ya?

q *shakes his head.*

C
(to p)

So what the fuck are you doing here?

P

We've been tailing your boss. He's a serial killer.

C

So.

P

So he's killed a couple of cops.

C *looks over his shoulder, towards the bar, then back at* P *and* Q.

C

You ready to deal now?

Q
(pleading)

Yeah, just get us the fuck outta here, man.

C

Okay, I'll give him to you guys if you promise not to charge me 'n' the kid for the murders. It was all his idea anyway. I mean, we just burned the bodies — that's all.

Q *looks over at* P *and begins sobbing.*

P
(swallowing hard)

Deal.

A *returns to the table with a round of beers. He puts the beers down in the centre of the table, then notices the sobbing* Q.

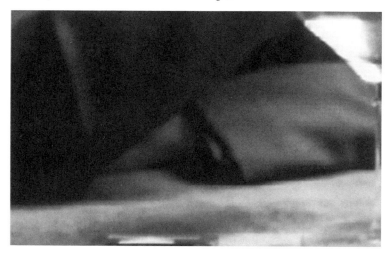

A

What the fuck's the matter with him?

C

Actor's workshop.

A
(*raising his eyebrows*)

Hey, he's pretty good.

P *bursts out laughing. It is a nervous laugh.*

A *gives* P *a funny look.*

A
(*to* C)

Him too?

C *nods.*

A *claps his hands together.*

A
(*looking around the table*)

Okay. Are we ready to play *Let's Make A Deal?*

The laughing P *and the sobbing* Q *both nod.*

A

Alright then.

A *notices* B *is gone from the table. He looks towards the washrooms, away from* C.

A
(*turning back towards* C)

Where'd that fuckin' kid —

C *grabs one of the beers, stands up, and smashes it over* A*'s head.*

A *looks stunned.*

A

Where?

Q*'s sobs turn into shrieks. He is losing it.*

P *gets up and runs.*

C *picks up another beer and smashes it over* Q*'s head.*

Q *falls over, still shrieking.*

A *is still standing, looking stunned.*

A
(wobbly)

Actor's workshop?

C *picks up another beer and smashes it over* A*'s head.*

A gun shot rings out in the distance.

C *picks up yet another beer. And with all his might, he smashes it over* A*'s head.*

A *slowly leans to his side and collapses.*

C *walks out of frame.*

A beat.

A second gun shot rings out.

Camera pans left.

TABLE FOUR

W2*'s head is bowed. She looks worn from crying.* W1 *has assumed a understanding posture.*

W1
(softly)

Have you talked to your father since he beat you up?

W2
(to the ashtray)

No.

W1

Has he tried getting in touch with you?

W2

No.

W1

Have you tried getting in touch with him?

A beat.

W2

Just my mom. A couple of times. She never answers the phone, though. I always get the answering machine.

W1

Have you left them messages?

W2

Yeah, but – I know them. They've cut me off. They're like that. They're fucked. My father's always been like that. He just freaks out, then he shuts off.

W1

Has he done stuff like this before? Hit you like that?

W2

Yeah. He's always been like that. He used to beat the shit out of my mom all the time when I was a kid.

W1

Did you ever try and get help? You know, phone a hotline or –

W2

No.

A siren sounds in the distance.

W1

What about the police?

W2
(*looking up*)

You gotta be kidding.

W1

Well, what about — you're Catholic, right? What about your priest?

w2 *scoffs, then looks away.*

W1

Friends?

W2

No.

W1

Oh.

A beat.

W1

What about the guy who got you pregnant?

w2 *makes a face.*

W1

Well, he was the father of your —

W2
(*turning back, angrily*)

The father of what?

W1

The father of —

W2
(*hostile*)

So what? What difference does that make?

W1

Well, I don't know. I just thought you might have told him.

W2

Hey, it's my body. He's got nothing to do with it. I mean – what's the point? I probably would've had an abortion, anyway.

W1

Yeah, but don't you think he has the right to know.

W2

Forget it. I don't think anybody has a right to know what goes on inside my body unless I tell them.

W1

Well, yeah, I agree. It's your choice. I mean, I'm pro-choice and all. But I just think that if somebody else is involved in something that's happening to you, like getting pregnant, then I think that they should be told. I mean – who knows? – at the very least they could help you through it.

W2 *scoffs.*

W1

But it's not like they have a right to influence your decision.

W2

Yeah, but they always do. Even if they agree with you, they always leave some kind of mark on you – a comment or something. And when they disagree, they leave you with a guilt trip. I mean – look at you. Judging by the age of your kids, it's pretty obvious you got married because you got pregnant, right?

W1

Yes, but we both wanted to get married. We were gonna get married anyway, so –

W2

Yeah, but the difference is you got married because you were pregnant. I mean, you might have been in love and everything, and you might have gotten married eventually –

W 1

No, no, no. We were different —

W 2

Or then again, if you waited, you might *not* have gotten married. You might have broken up. Then maybe your life would've been different. Maybe you would have gone to Liberia to —

W 1

Well, yeah. I see what you're saying. But no. I don't have any regrets. I loved my husband when I married him and I love the children we had together.

W 2

Yeah, but what if you married somebody else? What if you had kids with *them?* Maybe you'd be just as happy? Or happier? Or what if you never got married at all? Maybe you'd be happier.

W 1

No, I wouldn't.

W 2

How can you say that? You don't know.

W 1

I know I don't know. But there's no point in talking like this. It's not solving anything.

A beat.

W 2

Well, then there's no point in telling me that I shoulda told that guy I was pregnant.

W 1

No, that's different.

W 2

I don't see how.

                                W1
Well, I just think it is.

                                W2
But it isn't. I mean — look, what if I did? What if I told him I was
pregnant? And what if he wanted me to have the baby? What if he
tried to take me to court to have the baby? Or what if he didn't
want the baby? What if he was a real shit about it? What if I told
him I was pregnant and that I was going to get an abortion and
take care of it myself? And what if he told me to go fuck off,
anyway? Or what about this: What if I told him I was pregnant and
I was going to have an abortion? And what if he said something
like, «Okay, it's your body. I respect that. Here's the money. Good
luck.» I mean — that sounds ideal, right? But that would've fucked
me up just as bad. Because it's information. And it doesn't matter
if it's good or bad or whatever. It's just one more thing that'll get
lodged in my brain, one more distraction, one more pebble in my
shoe that I'll have to walk around with for the rest of my life. So
either way it's a fuck-up.

                                W1
Yeah, but that's life. That's what it's all about.

w2 *shakes her head.*

A beat.

                                W1
Getting pregnant — and making decisions about that pregnancy —
is something that happens all the time. I mean — what you've just
said has more to do with fear than anything else. And the sooner
you come to terms with that, the sooner you'll realize it's not such
a big deal.

                                W2
                            (*incredulous*)
Excuse me? And fear's not a big deal?

W 1

Well, yeah. But I try not to think about it.

W 2

Because you're scared.

W 1

Well —

W 2
(*sarcastically*)

What about denial? Do you try not to think about that, too?

W 1 *extends her hand to cover* W 2 *'s.*

W 1
(*compassionately*)

Hey, it's okay…

W 2 *relaxes her shoulders, looks away.*
(*whispering*)

…you're just scared.

W 2

Sure, whatever. So I'm scared. So what? Don't you ever get —

W 1

There's nothing to be scared of.

W 2 *slowly turns towards* W 1. W 2 *is crying, but her voice is unwavering.*

W 2

I disagree. I totally disagree. There's everything to be scared of.
Look at it out there. The whole world's a fuckin' mess. The
country's goin' down the tubes. Everybody's walking around in a
fuckin' daydream.…I have every reason to be scared. Every right.

> W1
> (*shrugs*)

Well, you just can't let that bother you. You've just got to put all
that aside and carry on with your life. Try to focus on the good
things. Stay positive —

> W2

And I will. I will carry on. But I'll carry on scared. And there's not
a single fuckin' thing you can say or do to make me feel otherwise.
Not one...single...fuckin'...thing.

W2 *finishes her drink.*

W1 *is unfazed.*

The squelch of a police walkie-talkie is heard.

*A cop and a detective enter the frame. They confer with each other facing
the camera but not looking into it.*

Camera begins a final 360-degree pan to the right.

TABLE ONE

Police and paramedics hover over the carnage.

TABLE TWO

Empty.

TABLE THREE

SHE *is lying on the floor, ignored.*

TABLE FOUR

Empty.

To black.

Afterword

THREE MONTHS AGO I received a call from Romulus Arnor, the editor and publisher of the Paris-based film journal, *Taynik*, asking me if I'd like to review Monika's Herendy's latest film, *American Whiskey Bar*. Not being much of a Herendy fan I said no. But Rom insisted. He said that the film (which, to my knowledge, had neither been released nor was slated for release) was causing a huge stir in Paris, and that the word on the street was that it was never going to be shown publicly. This time I laughed. I told Rom that I wasn't in the habit of reviewing films not intended for public view (what's the point, right?) and that maybe he should send someone else.

But Rom wouldn't have it. He said the film's producer had specifically invited me to a special screening. Not only that, *Taynik* was willing to fly me to Paris and pay me $5,000 (US) for the review. Laughing, I asked Rom what mental hospital he was calling from. Rom took the question literally. (A funny man, I could always tell when Rom was serious. This time he was serious.) In a firm voice he told me that the only thing he knew for sure was an address, a time, and the cheque in front of him with my name on it. Curious – and starving – I caught the next plane to Paris.

Rom was there to pick me up. He seemed particularly nervous. «We have less than three hours to make it to Rouen. Klaus changed locations at the last minute. If we boot it, we'll make it,» he said, yanking my bag off the carousel. Hmm. Strange behaviour, I thought. «Why are you acting so weird, Rom? And who's this Klaus guy?» I shouted after him, as he deked his way through the crowd. But Rom didn't answer. I tried again — a little louder. This time he swung around, the bag taking the legs out from under an elderly nun. As I helped the nun to her feet, Rom explained to me that in the twenty-four hours since we'd last talked *American Whiskey Bar* had become too big for a private showing in Paris, that the word was out, and that the producer, Klaus, had to find a secret location. That's why we were going to Rouen. I looked at him, incredulous. He stared back, his eyes bulging with urgency. Oh, Rom!

We were nearing the exit when we were approached by two young men in retro suits. «Excusez-moi, monsieur. Avez-vous, uh, voir *American Whiskey Bar?*» the smaller one asked, in bad French. Rom shot them a nasty look. Then the taller one began to say something unintelligible. Rom threw the bag over his shoulder, then shot the same look at me. His face radiated blame. I shrugged. Then Rom flipped out. Turning back to the young men he told them (in even worse French) that, no, he hadn't seen *American Whiskey Bar,* that just like everyone else in Paris he was never going to see *American Whiskey Bar,* and if they wouldn't mind just fucking off he could get started on what was turning out to be a very long trip to…to…to…*Port Bou!* But Rom's outburst hardly fazed the young suits. They stood their ground. In fact, every time Rom had said the words *American Whiskey Bar* more and more people in the airport stopped to listen in, until all you could hear was the hum of the baggage carousels. Rom then grabbed my arm and sped me towards the exit. All I could think about was how hard it is to run when you're laughing your head off.

It was only when we got into the car did I notice we were being followed. From his tone, Rom seemed to have known all along. «We're fucked,» he said, turning the key. «We might as well forget the whole fucking thing.» Just then, out of nowhere, a group of Vietnamese school girls threw themselves on the hood of the Citroën. «AM-ER-I-CAN

WHISK-EY BAR! AM-ER-I-CAN WHISK-EY BAR!» they chanted, their little fists pounding each syllable onto the windshield. Rom threw the car into reverse, turning sharply. The girls rolled over like netted fish. «What the fuck are you doing?!» I screamed. But Rom ignored me, throwing the car forward, screeching towards yet another exit. «Don't you realize what you've just done?» he huffed, as we pulled up to the pay booth. I looked behind me, expecting to see something flashing. «This is the most important film of the century, and you might have blown any chance of seeing it,» he said, passing the attendant a crumpled bill. I was about to say something like I was sorry, that I wish I could understand, but Rom's palm was already on the stick-shift. I braced myself instead.

Rom settled down once we got away from the airport, once he realized we were no longer being followed. I asked him what the hell was going on, what was all the fuss over a stupid movie? Rom took a drag off his cigarette, then tilted back his head, letting the smoke find its own way out of his mouth.

I waited. Rom chuckled, expelling the last of the smoke. He took a quick glance at the rear-view. Then he told me.

The story begins on a Sunday. The last Sunday of March, 1997. Rom is in his office laying out the next issue of *Taynik* when the phone rings. Because he was expecting a call from an advertiser, he answers. The voice is heavily accented. It is a German speaking French. Rom, the polyglot, immediately asks the caller to speak German. The voice asks to speak with the editor. Rom identifies himself. The voice introduces itself as Klaus 9. Within seconds Rom finds the voice too creepy, the questions too cryptic, then hangs up. Exactly one week later Rom is in the office finishing the layout when the phone rings. Rom is expecting a call from the Müllmanner Media Group, a Germany company that, a few days before, offered to buy out the fledgling *Taynik*. Rom picks up the phone and listens. Two minutes later Rom has sold *Taynik* for the outrageous sum of $500,000 (us). Rom is over the moon.

An hour later, just as Rom is finishing up, he hears a knock at the door. Because Rom is expecting a courier, he answers. Three well-dressed men enter the office. The older one, a gruff-looking man of about fifty, throws a briefcase over the reception desk, flicks open the locks, and pulls back the lid. Inside is a neat arrangement of hundred dollar (us) bills. Then the younger one, who looks barely twenty, approaches Rom with a manila folder, stopping just short of knocking him over. Rom steps back. The younger man, who, up close, is more earnest than threatening, hands Rom what looks to be a set of legal documents. Rom guesses right. They are the contracts for the sale of *Taynik*. Finally, the third man, who splits the difference age-wise among the three, and who looks thoroughly bored with the proceedings, reaches into his pocket and tosses Rom a pen. He tells Rom, in German, that if he signs the contracts he can have everything right now.

Now, Rom is no dummy. He calls up his lawyer and asks him to come over and read the contracts. His lawyer, Matthias, who is actually a mutual friend, and someone we've both known since our days in film school, arrives a short time later with a young intern, an attractive Senegalese woman named Patrice. The two of them retreat to the production room with the contracts. In the meantime, Rom waits in the reception area with what turns out to be the three vice-presidents of the Müllmanner Media Group. Rom feels awkward as the older vice-president begins to talk about film. He thinks the guy is an idiot. Then he feels scared. He thinks: I hope this guy isn't going to be involved in the editorial. But he thinks again: well, so fucking what if he is? It's their magazine, they can do whatever they want.

About an hour later Rom hears the scuff of chairs coming from the production room. Thank god, Rom thinks. The older vp was driving Rom insane with his imbecilic porno survey. The door opens a peek. A dour Patrice asks Rom if he would like to step inside. For a second Rom feels like a patient whose about to be told some bad news. Rom enters the production room, sits down, and is told by Matthias that the contract is a sound offer, that Rom will be retained as editor at the sum of $60,000 (us) per year, and that, considering the magazine isn't even worth one-percent of the Müllmanner Media Group's offer, Rom should sign. Rom agrees. Matthias then calls for a vp with signing authority. The older man signs on behalf of the company. Through the open door of the production room Rom notices the middle-man listening on a cellphone.

No sooner is the deal done when the office door flies open. A large, caped, middle-aged man blusters in with a kite-tail of scene-stars behind him. Rom thinks the man looks like a cross between a bürgermeister he once saw in a portrait show in Köln and a wwf wrestler. The man walks past his vps and looks hard at Matthias. Matthias nods politely, acknowledging the big man's presence. Rom, intimidated by the big man (but at the same time proprietary), introduces himself to the group, asking them if they're lost. The group giggles. The big man smiles. «On the contrary, I'm feeling right at home,» he says, to more giggles. Rom offers his hand in another effort to introduce himself. But the big man ignores him, turning towards the middle-man, removing a copy of the contract from his lap. He flips through a couple of pages, then stops, tossing the contract back at the middle-man. «Contracts,» he begins, «aren't even worth the paper they're written on. But I like you, Rom. And we're going to have a good time with this magazine.» The big man smiles, extending a fat hand to Rom, introducing himself as the president of the Müllmanner Media Group, Klaus 9.

We were making good time. We arrived in Rouen with a few minutes to spare. Rom pulled up in front of an Algerian café, a dumpy place called Souk's. «C'mon, I'll buy you a coffee,» he said, checking his watch again. «This is where you'll meet Klaus 9.»

Once seated, Rom picked up the story.

There was a huge party in the *Taynik* office that Sunday. As soon as Rom and Klaus 9 shook hands, a team of white-uniformed caterers burst into the room, setting up tables and uncovering huge slabs of beef and cheese. An accordion player followed, squeezing out a polka version of The Smiths' «How Soon Is Now?» Then the popping of corks. The party went on all night. And Rom, who could be characterized as a frail man (but a man who loved a party), passed out somewhere between four or five in the morning. His last recollection was of Klaus 9 giving out hundred dollar (us) bills to various members of his entourage, for «outrageous acts of courage.»

When Rom awoke, he wondered whether it had all been a dream. He got up from under his desk and looked around. There was absolutely nothing to suggest there had been a party as raging as the one he barely remembered. The office was spotless. Everything was the way it had been when he arrived on the morning of the day before. Rom was so out of it he had to think for a minute whether or not he was hung over.

Then he saw it. The money. In exactly the same place it was first laid out. Untouched. The money brought everything back to him: the vice-presidents, Klaus 9, the caterers, the accordion player, the champagne. ... Rom was feeling woozy. Then he noticed something tucked under the lid of the briefcase. The contracts. He began to read them, but the legalese only made him woozier. He lay down on the reception room sofa and fell back to sleep.

Rom dreamed he went to New York to write for a new journal of film criticism, *Eagle Maniac*. Things went well at first, he was able to do what he wanted. He wrote damning essays on the Hollywood studio system as well as the films of the day. (One of his first pieces, an indictment of a *Pretty Woman*-type thing called *She Belongs To Me*, was republished in *Harper's*). About a year after starting at the journal (which had quintupled its circulation since Rom's arrival), *Eagle Maniac*'s publisher, the appropriately-named Miles Smiley, introduced Rom to a friend of his at PBS, a producer who was looking to start a film review show, something along the lines of *Siskel & Ebert*, but more high-brow. The producer, impressed with Rom's quick wit and stiff accent, thought the «Sprocket»-like Rom would «pair well» with another film critic, bell hooks. Rom was interested. So was hooks. Although the two grew to despise each other, the tension between them made great TV. The show lasted six months. Both vowed never to do TV again. Rom then returned to *Eagle Maniac* and took over the editorial. His first act was to change the name of the journal to its pet-name, *E-Mania*. About six weeks later, at the staff Christmas party, Smiley announced that the journal was being sold to a Hollinger subsidiary, but that everybody's job was secure.

The dream quickly turned into a nightmare. About a month after the buy-out, just as the first under-new-ownership issue hit the stands, Rom was passing by a kiosk when something caught his eye – the new *E-Mania*. But something was wrong. It wasn't the copy he edited. He grabbed the copy from the stand and held it before him. It seemed to be moving, like a hologram, one minute looking like *Time*, the next minute like *People*, the next minute like *Us*. . . . Rom was furious. Someone has ripped off our name, he thought. Then the newsstand attendant, recognizing Rom from TV, complimented him on the current issue. Rom was speechless. He flipped through the magazine. Articles that were so heavily down on Hollywood were now singing its praises. He felt nauseous. He flipped to the masthead. EDITOR: ROMULUS ARNOR. It felt as though his temples were being tapped with ball-peen hammers. He vomited.

Rom awoke from the dream to find the office under intense renovation. One of Klaus 9's entourage, a little Basque boy who introduced himself as Teddy, was wiping puke off the sofa. «Klaus wants to change everything but the sofa,» Teddy said, ringing the cloth out over a galvanized bucket. Rom asked where Klaus was. Teddy told him. Rom jumped from the sofa and staggered into his office, where Matthias was beating a pleading Patrice, while Klaus jerked off and shouted into a cellphone. Rom screamed so loud he woke himself up.

Rom was back on the sofa. Standing over him was Klaus 9. «You don't look so good,» said Klaus, puffing on a huge Cuban. Rom asked him if he would mind not smoking that thing. Insulted, Klaus told Rom to fuck off, that he owned the joint now, and that he could do whatever the fuck he wanted. Rom agreed, then looked over at the money – still in its same spot, still untouched. «Of course, what I said last night, Rom, just before you took your clothes off, still stands: you will have complete editorial control over *Taynik*; and my only interest in this magazine is in the publishing of one article, the review of Monika Herendy's new film *American Whiskey Bar*,» said Klaus, smiling through blue smoke. «Then, I will never bother you again.» Rom got up slowly, dragged himself over to the reception desk, and shut the lid on the money. «Okay,» Rom said. «No problem.»

Rom sat back, exhausted. I told him that was quite a story. Rom nodded. Then I began to think about my situation. Here I was, in Rouen, waiting to see a movie by a man who owns both the movie and the journal I'll be writing for. «Kinda unethical, don't you think?» I said, positively unwilling to put my reputation on the line. Rom shrugged. «Only if you don't like the movie,» he replied. I thought a bit more, then asked him if what he was saying was that Klaus only wanted to see a good review. Rom nodded. Hmm. «So it's basically like he's paid you $500,000 (US) for my $5,000 (US) endorsement?» I asked. Rom nodded. I then told Rom that whether or not I liked the film was entirely inconsequential to the economic disparity of the situation, given the fact that my reputation as a film critic was at least on par with *Taynik*'s reputation as a widely respected film voice. «True enough,» Rom said. «So you'll do it for, what, maybe, oh, a hundred grand?» he asked, the sparkle of his old self reflecting in his eye. «Do I have to use my own name?» I joked. «Yep,» said Rom.

Klaus 9 arrived just like Rom had described. And Rom was right: Klaus's presence was as huge as his entourage. «Ah, you must be Milena Jagoda,» Klaus bellowed, approaching me with open arms, then dropping to one knee. «I've brought with me my beautiful people,» he said, flicking a wrist their way. But I couldn't take my eyes off Klaus. He was one of the biggest men I'd ever seen. (Though crouched down beside us, Klaus still towered over the table. And when he bent over to kiss my hand, I honestly thought he was going to suck my fist into that enormous mouth of his and swallow me whole.) Klaus suggested we view the film as soon as possible, that they had been followed from Paris, and that he didn't want any trouble in a town where he had no influence. I laughed, not only because it all seemed so implausible, but because I was nervous. I looked over to Rom, as if to say «Let's go,» but Rom looked away. Klaus, who hadn't let go of my hand since the kiss, stood up, pulling me with him. «Rom won't be coming,» he said. «It's just you and me.»

I wanted to run for it, but I knew I'd never get away. Klaus kept a friendly grip on my arm, I knew he could break it just as quick. We walked to the end of the street where a man in Müllmanner coveralls was waiting by a metal door. He opened the door, slamming it shut as we walked through and made our way up the stairs. «Over here,» said Klaus, turning sharply to the right, where we met another man in coveralls, and another metal door. Same thing: we walked through and the door slammed behind us.

We were now in the viewing room. The only source of light was coming from the screen: a black doctor was being fellated by a young woman in a hospital gown while a nurse looked on. Klaus laughed as he pulled from his pants' pocket a remote control, fast-forwarding the scene to a test pattern. «From Herendy's documentary on Bulgarian prostitutes,» Klaus said, before pointing to a couple of large over-stuffed chairs on either side of the projector. I smiled weakly and sat down, scared. Klaus continued to stand, fiddling with the remote until the words KLAUS 9 PICTURES PRESENTS appeared on the screen, pausing the image, then sitting down himself. He placed the remote on the chair's arm and reached down for what turned out to be a briefcase. He opened the briefcase and pulled from it a single sheet of legal-sized paper, handing it to me, asking me to read it.

Now I was really scared. And I mean petrified. But I was angry, too. As much as I fought to hang on to my anger, I knew I could only lose – which made me more scared, more angry. For what Klaus handed me that night in Rouen was not so much a contract but a map – a map that I was doomed to follow. The contract stated that I would be paid the sum of $5,000 (US) for my review of *American Whiskey Bar*. It stipulated that I WAS NOT TO MENTION IN MY REVIEW OR ANYWHERE ELSE any details regarding plot, setting, dialogue, characters, or talent. It also stipulated that I was to write what would be construed as a good review. I turned to Klaus and told him I couldn't agree to this, that I couldn't allow myself to be comprised.... And as I told him this I thought back to my last conversation with Rom, just a few minutes earlier, how I joked with him (if only to rouse the flicker of his old self), and how my joke with him (although I didn't realize it at the time) was once again taken seriously; and how that seriousness was the new Rom, and that the funny Rom had died somewhere long ago.... And I kept thinking about this as I kept telling Klaus why I couldn't agree to his terms, as if what I had to say would somehow sink in, as if he would submit to my reasoning or – at the very least – give in out of complete exhaustion – even pity.

But I could see that Klaus was growing restless, that his body was preparing to shut me up. But I didn't care. I was too scared, too angry, I just wanted it to be over. The only way I was to sign this contract was if he took my hand and made me – which was what he did when he told me that he was sorry, that I had no choice, that he'd kill me if I didn't....

So, from the spring 1997 issue of *Taynik 9 Film Fun:*

> I am not accustomed to writing reviews about films that aren't made for public view. (What's the point, right?) However, in the case of *American Whiskey Bar,* I'm going to make an exception – if only because I can't recall an unreleased film causing so much huff, so much commotion as this one.
>
> So what is *American Whiskey Bar?* Well, it's a phenomenon, right? So it doesn't really matter what it's about. *It's a phenomenon.* It exists entirely outside of itself. It's importance has more to do with its consequences as a phenomenon than its definition as a « real » movie. And as anyone who is even remotely associated with the film industry (which, at last count, was nearing five billion people) knows, *American Whiskey Bar* is quite possibly the most consequential film of the twentieth century.

American Whiskey Bar was produced by Klaus 9. It was
directed by Monika Herendy, although she denies it. The
screenplay, which was based on an idea by Monika
Herendy, was written by a Canadian, Michael Turner.
Turner, depending on what mood he is in, sometimes
denies having anything to do with the film. The cine-
matographer and editor was the late Evgeny Churkin, who
died of a heroin overdose a short time after the film was
completed.

So how many people have seen *American Whiskey Bar?* I
would say, at this point, no more than twelve. Thirteen if
you include the film's producer (and gatekeeper), Klaus 9.

Klaus 9 shows the film privately, to select audiences of
no more than one person at a time. The people Klaus 9 has
shown the film to fall into two camps: those who deny
having seen it; and those who admit to having seen it, but
refuse to talk about it. The latter group, comprised mostly
of Hollywood's elite, allow you to tell them what you think
the film's about in exchange for the gratification that
invariably comes to them once they've told you you're
wrong. For this group the film has become a kind of
currency, a parlor game, a secret handshake that is
exchanged and played out in hot spots the world over.

I have seen *American Whiskey Bar.* And although I'd
like to say it's a horrible film, I can't. Not because it's a
great film, but because I am not philosophically disposed
to nominal distinctions. I can tell you this, though: *American Whiskey Bar* is one of the most disturbing portraits of
contemporary American society I have seen in some time:
a swirling mass of racist, sexist, classist bile — violent to
the core, yet strangely liberating; a rare blend of pairings,
where the grey areas that lurk between a range of seem-
ingly non-contradictory partnerships (ambition and
greed, desire and lust, compassion and patronage, regret
and regression, emphasis and exaggeration, lies and
expediencies . . .) are removed and further distilled, out

of which drop the silver beads of power over the tear stains of despair. And I love it.

But what's it about, though!? Well, I can't say. Not because I don't know (because I do), but because a condition of seeing this film was signing a release that forbade me from discussing any and all aspects of plot, setting, dialogue, characters, and talent. The only particulars I can comment on are the camera position, the length of the film, and the music. I can also say a few things about what this film is not.

So: *American Whiskey Bar* is shot with a single 35-millimetre camera. The camera is mounted on a tripod and is fixed in the middle of an area of activity, panning no more than thirty times throughout the two-hour-and-ten-minute film, making only three uninterrupted (360-degree) revolutions. With the exception of four or five cut-aways and a couple of closeups, *American Whiskey Bar* is one big master shot. A lone Hammond organ provides the soundtrack. None of the music is recognizable.

Notwithstanding the opening scene (a long, drawn-out establishing shot of a dimly-lit interior), *American Whiskey Bar* bears little resemblance to a Monika Herendy film. The characters are not engaged in long discussions of wheat harvests and draught animals, nor are they concerned with the black market interfering with the availability of vodka or cabbage heads. But like a Herendy film, these characters are divided into separate stories. However, unlike a Herendy film, these stories do not unite to form a neat narrative suture. This is not to imply that these stories are left dangling; it's just that some do, some don't, and some do so together.

Another thing that *American Whiskey Bar* isn't is a work of realism. Although its beginning shares a realism with Herendy's earlier films, *American Whiskey Bar* quickly veers into the fantastic. A character from another character's past appears out of nowhere and engages in a surreal sexual / political act with a second character that, at first, seems to have little bearing on the story (although we later attribute that moment to a transformation in the second character's character). The strength of this bizarre scene is such that it refocusses the viewers' readings of the other stories in the film, creating both an expectation from the banal (or the rhetorical) and a surrender to the implausible (or the unthinkable). The resulting dislocation is what makes *American Whiskey Bar* the film it is.

And that's all I can't say about that. I mean, I suppose I could talk about the riot last week in Prague, where all those young Czechs got trampled to death while waiting outside the B M W factory, where *American Whiskey Bar* was rumoured to have been showing. Or I could talk about the mysterious death of those five American college kids in Budapest, who were beaten to a pulp and thrown onto the steps of their embassy. I suppose I could make some kind of connection between those two events in order to illustrate the impact *American Whiskey Bar* is having here in Europe right now. But that's not really my job, is it? My job is to review films, right?

Now, I know what you might be thinking. You might be thinking, Oh, Milena. How could you? How could you do this to us? We who want to know. We who have trusted your criticism for so long. And for that I am truly sorry, I really am. But what would you expect me to do!? I was broke. I had no resources. And despite the fact that I make my living writing about films, I was curious. I had to see it for myself. I had to see what all the fuss was about. I had to see it to protect you, my dear readers, from that which you might believe this movie is, from that which you might have heard from someone else. And I think it was worth it (don't you?) that I entered into an agreement with the film's producer, that I am keeping mum on the contents of *American Whiskey Bar*. I mean, I'm not like those evil Hollywood types; I'm not going to stand here smug and tell you what you think you know is wrong. On the contrary, my dear readers, I assure you that I will continue to go out of my way to tell you, if ever you want me to – at any time, at any place, wherever you may be – everything this movie has done, everything this movie is capable of doing, and, for as long as I live, everything this movie is not.

Milena Jagoda

1997

MICHAEL TURNER is the author of *Company Town*, *Hard Core Logo*, *Kingsway*, and *The Pornographer's Poem*. His work has been adapted to radio, stage, television, and feature film, and translated into French, Russian, and Korean. He lives in Vancouver, where, in addition to books and screenplays, he writes art essays.

photo. Brian Jungen